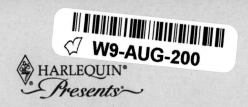

With Valentine's Day, February is always a romantic month. And we've got some great books in store for you....

The High-Society Wife by Helen Bianchin is the story of a marriage of convenience between two rich and powerful families.... But what this couple didn't expect is for their marriage to become real! It's also the first in our new miniseries RUTHLESS, where you'll find commanding men, who stop at nothing to get what they want. Look out for more books coming soon! And if you love Italian men, don't miss *The Marchese's Love-Child* by Sara Craven, where our heroine is swept off her feet by a passionate tycoon.

If you just want to get away from it all, let us whisk you off to the beautiful Greek Islands in Julia James's hard-hitting story *Baby of Shame.* What will happen when a businessman discovers that his night of passion with a young Englishwoman five years ago resulted in a son? The Caribbean is the destination for our couple in Anne Mather's intriguing tale *The Virgin's Seduction.*

Jane Porter has a dangerously sexy Sicilian for you in *The Sicilian's Defiant Mistress.* This explosive reunion story promises to be dark and passionate! In Trish Morey's *Stolen by the Sheikh,* the first in her new duet, THE ARRANGED BRIDES, a young woman is summoned to the palace of a demanding sheikh, who has plans for her future.... Don't miss part two, coming in March.

See the inside front cover for a list of titles and book numbers.

Kathryn Ross

A SPANISH ENGAGEMENT

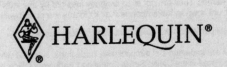

TORONTO • NEW YORK • LONDON
AMSTERDAM • PARIS • SYDNEY • HAMBURG
STOCKHOLM • ATHENS • TOKYO • MILAN • MADRID
PRAGUE • WARSAW • BUDAPEST • AUCKLAND

ISBN 0-373-18868-4

A SPANISH ENGAGEMENT

First North American Publication 2006.

Copyright © 2003 by Kathryn Ross.

This edition published by arrangement with Harlequin Books S.A.

www.eHarlequin.com

Printed in U.S.A.

All about the author...
Kathryn Ross

KATHRYN ROSS was born in Zambia to an English father and an Irish mother. She was educated in Ireland and England, where she later worked as a professional beauty therapist before becoming a full-time writer.

Most of her childhood was spent in a small village in southern Ireland; she said it was a wonderful place to grow up surrounded by the spectacular beauty of the Wicklow Mountains and the rugged coastline of the Irish Sea. She feels that living in Ireland first sparked off her desire to write; it was so rich in both scenery and warm characters that it literally invited her to put pen to paper.

Kathryn loves to travel and seek out exotic locations for her books. She feels it helps her writing to be able to set her scenes against backgrounds that she has visited. Traveling and meeting people also give her great inspiration to start all her novels; she gets a spark of excitement from some incident or conversation and that sets her imagination working. Her characters are always a pastiche of different people she has either met or read about, or would like to meet. She likes being a novelist because she can make things happen—well, most of the time anyhow. Sometimes her characters take over and do things that even surprise her!

At present Kathryn is working on her next book, and can be found walking her dogs in the Lake District in England as she thinks about her plots.

To my mother, Hazel, and my sister, Lesley,
with love and thanks.

CHAPTER ONE

IT WAS strange how life could change in an instant, Carrie thought as she took her place in the business-class section of the plane. At one time when she was on a business trip to the Paris office she would have lingered after the meetings to enjoy a spot of shopping on the Champs-Elysées. Or she would have met up with colleagues for a drink. These days she couldn't really care less about all that—all she could think about was getting home on time to be with her niece.

Carrie checked her wrist-watch as the pilot apologised for their delayed departure and said that their estimated time of arrival in Barcelona was four-thirty.

It was touch and go now whether she would be home in time to pick Molly up from school herself. Usually it wouldn't have mattered because she employed a nanny as backup. But Silvia had asked for time off this week due to personal problems, and the girl had looked so pale and miserable that Carrie had felt obliged to agree. Somehow she had managed to juggle appointments around and had been able to pick Molly up herself all week. It had been hard work, but despite this she had really enjoyed it. In fact, the highlight of her day was when her niece came running out of class, her dark curls bouncing, and a big smile on her face. The warmth of her welcome and the way she flung herself into Carrie's arms for a hug never failed to move her.

Carrie was a successful advertising executive and she was used to life in the fast lane, but she had to admit that in the last few months since Molly had come to live with

7

her her priorities had undergone a serious overhaul. Suddenly her career was no longer the most important thing in her life. And for Carrie that was a massive change. She had always been career-driven, the first to arrive in the office in the morning and last to leave at night. It was that total dedication that had earned her a top job in the agency's office in Barcelona. But these days she couldn't wait to get home, and she found instead of wanting to read business reports in the evening she was more likely to be found reading bedtime stories to Molly.

Colleagues in the office were starting to notice the change…and she knew it wasn't going down too well with her immediate superior either. Her job was high-pressured, but also highly prized, and there were a lot of people who were just waiting for her to trip up.

But Carrie didn't intend to make any errors. Even though she had been pushed to the limits timewise this week, she had won a lot of new contracts, proving she was still on top of her job. So she didn't care much what anyone thought. Molly needed her and that was all that mattered.

It was three months now since the tragic accident that had robbed the little girl of her father and Carrie hadn't hesitated to take her in. What else could she have done? Molly was her half-brother's child and there were no other living relatives except for grandparents who were currently in Australia, and whom Molly hardly knew.

One look at the child sitting in the police station waiting for her, looking bewildered and frightened, and Carrie had rushed to sign the forms that would release her into her care. And even though it had caused all kinds of complications in her life—with work, with her social life, which was now practically non-existent—Carrie didn't regret it; in fact she had made an application to legally adopt the child a few weeks ago. She had thought that it would just be a formality, and that by Christmas Molly would legally be hers. But a few days ago she had received an ominous letter from Molly's grandmother stating she wasn't happy about the idea and wanted to come and see her.

She was due to arrive tomorrow night and Carrie was more than a little anxious about the visit. Trying to put those worries out of her mind, she opened up her briefcase and tried to turn her attention back to work.

Tomorrow was Friday and there was a whole day's work to get through before she had to think about Molly's grandmother. It was an important day as well, because she wanted to win the contract for advertising Santos Wines. She had come up with some good ideas at the office meeting last week, and her boss José had told her to go ahead and develop them but she knew he was starting to watch her performance with critical eyes. The real test would be if she could sell her ideas to the managers of the Santos estate at their meeting tomorrow.

Carrie's mind was filled with facts and figures when a man took his seat beside her. She looked up, prepared to smile politely before going back to the papers in front of her. But something happened when she looked into his dark eyes...suddenly her very businesslike frame of mind was severely shaken. The man was absolutely gorgeous.

She tried to focus back on her work but she found herself distracted by his presence. She was aware of the long, lean, powerful body just centimetres away from hers in a way that she had never experienced before. Never in her whole life had she felt such an overwhelming attraction to a man. Even the subtle tang of his aftershave sent her senses reeling.

Every now and then she darted surreptitious glances towards him, taking in everything about him: the ruggedly handsome profile, the thick darkness of his hair, the cut of his expensive suit, even his hands that were large and capable-looking. She noticed as well the way the air stewardesses smiled at him as they passed. This was a man who was used to being noticed by women, she decided; so in response she tried very hard to ignore him.

For take-off she had to put her papers away and tuck her briefcase beneath the seat in front. As the plane roared down the runway she put her hand on the armrest of her seat and accidentally brushed against his hand.

'Sorry.' She looked over at him and he smiled at her. It had the weirdest effect on her body, as if her heart had dipped in some weightless way down into her stomach and back again. She gave a polite half-smile and hurriedly looked away again, hating the fluttery sensation he was stirring inside her. Carrie liked to be in control of her senses at all times and this was pure purgatory for her.

Pull yourself together, for heaven's sake, she told herself sharply. You're a twenty-nine-year-old businesswoman, not a blushing adolescent.

As the plane levelled out she reached to open her briefcase again and got out her papers. She felt his glance falling on her as she tried to read, and was acutely aware that he seemed to be studying her rather intently. She wished now that she hadn't drawn her long blonde hair back into such a severe style this morning—she could have done with the silky curtain to hide behind.

'Are you going to Barcelona on business?' he asked her suddenly.

'No, I live there. I'm returning from a business trip.' She noticed the huskily attractive Spanish accent. That accounted for the blue-black colour of his hair and the penetrating dark eyes, she thought. 'What about you?' she asked, unable to contain her curiosity. 'Do you live in Barcelona or are you on business as well?'

'A little of both.' He smiled.

Although her curiosity was rife she refrained from asking what he did for a living. It was obvious he was successful at whatever it was; he had an air of authority about him that spoke volumes. Instead she tried to reapply herself to her work, but found that she was reading the same paragraph over and over again. Her mind stubbornly refused to concentrate on what was important; instead it was focusing on him—on his every move, his every word.

She listened as he chatted amiably with one of the hostesses in Spanish. She had thought his English accent was sexy but it was nothing compared to the warm, deep tones of his native tongue. Although Carrie was English by birth she was multi-lingual and spoke Spanish fluently so she had no problem following the conversation. The hostess was flirting outrageously with him, and he didn't seem too averse to the attention. In fact he seemed to be flirting right back. Little wonder, really, Carrie thought; the woman was dark and Spanish and very attractive.

Carrie frowned down at the papers in front of her and told herself to stop listening. She didn't care what he was doing. It was none of her business; all that mattered to her was that she got this contract with Santos Wines tomorrow. And if she did her homework now she would have time to spring-clean her apartment tonight and prepare for meeting Molly's grandmother tomorrow.

'Would you like a drink?' he asked her suddenly, and she looked up to see the air stewardess waiting to take her order.

She was tempted to accept, but smiled and shook her head regretfully. 'Thank you, but I can't. I have to concentrate on this work.'

'Very sensible.' He smiled back.

Hell, but he had a gorgeous smile, Carrie thought hazily.

The plane lurched suddenly and some of her papers

slipped sideways off her table, falling onto the floor at his feet. He retrieved them for her immediately.

'Thanks.' Her hand touched his accidentally as she took them from him and she felt suddenly breathless. What was wrong with her? she wondered dreamily. She had met lots of good-looking men over the years and not one of them had ever affected her like this.

'Do you work for Santos Wines?' he asked as he glanced down at the logo on one of the papers.

'Not exactly. I work for an advertising agency and I'm hoping to run a series of advertisements on TV for their wines.'

'Really? Now, that is interesting. Their wine is excellent.'

'Is it?' Carrie grinned suddenly and something made her lower her normal barriers of reserve to confess, 'Actually, I've never tried it...although I probably shouldn't admit to that.'

'Probably not.' He gave her a lopsided, boyishly attractive grin that made her heart skip.

Irritated with herself for responding to him like that, she tried to remain businesslike. 'But I'll be able to sell it no matter what it tastes like. I'm pretty good at thinking up new and innovative ideas for any product, good or bad. That's my job.'

'But doesn't it help you if you believe in the product?'

'Yes, of course.' Carrie nodded hastily. 'And I'll be learning all about Santos Wines tomorrow. I'm visiting one of their vineyards and talking with the producers.'

His eyes flicked down over her, suddenly taking in everything about her, from the smart way her blonde hair was tied back from her face to the black skirt suit and round-neck white top.

Carrie felt her blood heating up at the way he was looking at her. It was almost as if he were touching her with his eyes.

'Well, anyway, if you'll excuse me...' She wrenched her eyes away from him. 'I'd better get back to my work.'

'Of course.' He nodded politely and she wondered if she had imagined the gleam of sexual interest in his eyes a moment ago.

The air stewardess arrived with his drink and Carrie focused rigidly on her work as some more conversation flowed in Spanish.

A little while later a meal was served and she was forced to put her papers away. It was strange, but she felt totally vulnerable without them in front of her. She couldn't pretend that she wasn't in the slightest bit affected by him, couldn't escape from the disturbing, powerful sensuality of the man.

'So how's the work going?' he asked as she took out her cutlery and studiously pretended to be interested in her food.

'It's going okay, thank you,' she said awkwardly.

'That's good.'

The stewardess arrived with a bottle of wine. 'Ah, now you can't refuse a glass of this,' he said with a smile. And she noticed he had ordered a bottle of Santos white wine. 'You can mix business with pleasure now, and do a bit of research.'

'That's very kind of you...but...'

'Not really. I have an ulterior motive,' he said, cutting across her casually as he poured the wine.

'What kind of motive?' she said, glancing across at him uncertainly.

'Well, I want to know if you actually like the stuff.' He grinned at her. 'I know you said it wouldn't make any difference to your advertising campaign. But...' he shrugged in a very Hispanic way '...I'm curious to find out the truth.'

She carefully avoided touching his hand as she took the glass he offered. He watched as she took a small sip, his eyes moving slowly over her delicate heart-shaped face, noting the high cheekbones, the generous curve of her lips. He noticed that she didn't wear much make-up—not that she needed it particularly. Her skin was exquisite and her large baby-blue eyes needed no enhancement at all.

'Well?'

Carrie waited a moment for the flavour to develop in her mouth. 'It's very refreshing...slightly fruity, not too dry...' She took another sip. 'Yes, it's very good,' she admitted. 'Not that I'm a connoisseur or anything, but I would recommend it to a friend so I guess I'll have no problem with my conscience when I'm selling it...that's if I get the advertising contract.' She hastily qualified her words, not wanting to tempt fate. 'Nothing is certain yet.'

He poured himself a glass and raised it towards hers in a salute. 'So tell me a little about your agency. Is it big or small?'

'It's called *Images* and it's very big. They have offices in London, New York, Paris and Madrid, and twelve months ago opened the one in Barcelona which is where I now work. It's been quite a challenge building it up, and we are getting some really good contracts so it's expanding rapidly.'

'I take it they transferred you from the London office?'

'Yes. I was relocated out here with my boss, José. And then we hired staff locally. It's a great post—I'm really enjoying living in Barcelona.'

'It's a beautiful city,' he agreed. 'I'm always happy to return.'

Who was he returning to? Carrie wondered. If sensuality could be measured on a scale of one to ten, he'd be off the scale.

To cover her sudden feeling of awkwardness she continued hastily, 'So if you ever need any advertising for your business, you'll have to keep *Images* in mind.' Was she babbling? she wondered suddenly. She never usually felt like this around men. She was always coolly in control—in fact so much so that she knew it had sometimes irritated her boyfriends.

'I'll definitely bear you in mind.' He smiled. 'What are your ideas for the Santos Wines company?'

She hesitated before answering that question.

'I'm not in the advertising business,' he assured her with a grin.

'What business are you in?' she asked, suddenly aware that he seemed to be asking her a lot of questions.

'I'm a lawyer.'

'Really?' She paused for a moment, and felt like asking him if he knew anything about adoption laws, then pulled herself back. It was one thing discussing her work, quite another launching into a discussion about Molly with a total stranger.

She was surprised he was a lawyer; he didn't look as if he worked indoors. He had a wonderful physique. She wondered if he worked out in a gym—it wasn't that he was overly muscular, but he just seemed extremely fit. She gauged him to be about six years older than her, about thirty-five or six, but he obviously looked after himself. His body was very well honed.

'I work in corporate law, so it's mostly big businesses that I deal with.'

'Oh, I see.' She nodded, glad she had refrained from asking him about her dilemma. Not that it was going to be too much of a problem, she assured herself hastily. Once she met Molly's grandmother and allayed her fears, the adoption would probably go ahead without any problems.

'We should introduce ourselves,' he said smoothly. 'I'm Max.'

'Carrie Michaels.'

He smiled. 'Pleased to meet you, Carrie.'

The air stewardess came along to collect the trays, leaving them with just the bottle of wine between them.

'So, you were telling me of your plans for Santos Wines,' he prompted gently.

He looked genuinely interested and Carrie found herself expanding on her ideas. 'Well, it's a family business and I thought we should work on that angle.' She took out a rough childish drawing that Molly had scribbled on one of her business papers last week. 'This gave me the idea, actually.'

He took the drawing and studied it intently. It was of matchstick figures dancing through what looked like vines with a big yellow sun above their heads.

'Very artistic.' He grinned. 'Is it all your own work?'

She smiled. 'My four-year-old niece did it last week. I wasn't too happy at the time, but then I looked at it and thought…that's it—it's perfect. Santos Wines need to change their image and expand on the idea of the family, and at the same time make it young and trendy.'

He was very easy to talk to and he asked very pertinent questions—questions she was sure the director of the company would ask when she went to meet with him tomorrow.

It wasn't until the seat-belt sign came on and the pilot told them they were preparing to land that she realised just how much talking she had done.

'That time seemed to go very quickly…' she murmured. 'I hope I haven't been boring you too much about my work.'

'On the contrary, I've found it fascinating.'

She wondered if he was being very polite. Nobody could really have been as genuinely interested in the subject of advertising wine as he seemed to be.

The flight touched down smoothly and Carrie felt a pang of regret that she hadn't found out much about him. He had been adroit at drawing her out but very reserved when it came to revealing things about himself, she realised.

The seat-belt sign went out and as everyone stood up to collect their belongings she noticed how tall he was—well over six feet two.

She glanced at her watch, trying to close her mind to him. He was just a passing stranger; they would probably never see each other again. What was more important was the time. She should just about make it to the school for Molly.

'It's been a very interesting flight. I've enjoyed your company,' he said casually as she stood up and gathered her belongings.

'Yes, me too...'

He stood back and allowed her to precede him off the plane. Carrie noticed that the air stewardess only had eyes for him as they passed at the door.

Curiously Carrie glanced back and noticed she had put a detaining hand on his shoulder and was saying something to him.

Probably something along the lines of, Would you like to take my number? Carrie thought dryly.

For a moment she was reminded forcibly of her ex-husband. He'd been like that; everywhere they had gone women had fallen over themselves to get his attention...it hadn't even seemed to matter that she was with him.

The memory made her keep on walking without looking back.

The heat of the Spanish sun hit her as she stepped out of the aircraft and onto the steps. The sky was an amazingly clear azure blue, and the breeze that ruffled her hair was dry with dust from the arid ground that blew over the runways.

It didn't take long to clear Immigration; Carrie just held up her passport as she walked through into the modern airport. She had no luggage to collect so she went straight outside.

Usually there were plenty of taxis waiting outside the terminal, but today there was only one. Hurriedly she made her way in its direction, only to notice that there was already a passenger in the back seat. He turned slightly as she approached and she noticed it was the man who had sat next to her on the plane. How on earth had he got out here so quickly? she wondered in surprise.

He opened the door just as she was about to walk away. 'You look like you're in a hurry,' he said. 'Do you want to share this taxi with me?'

Carrie looked into those meltingly dark attractive eyes and for a moment she hesitated; then, remembering Molly sitting in the classroom waiting for her, she nodded. 'Thanks.' She smiled at him as she climbed into the vehicle beside him. 'Do you mind dropping me off first? You're right—I am in a hurry. I'm on the last minute before picking my niece up from school.'

'Of course,' he acceded easily, and then listened as she gave the driver the address.

'Thank you,' she said politely to him again, and relaxed back into the seat beside him.

'That's okay. I'm going out to the other side of the city anyway, so you are practically on the way.'

Carrie got her mobile phone out to ring one of her friends who had kindly said she would pick Molly up for her if she were delayed today. 'Hi, Bernadette, it's Carrie.

It's okay, I don't need you to pick Molly up from school. I'll be a few minutes late but I will be there.'

As she listened to Bernadette's light-hearted rejoinder, Carrie's eyes drifted to the man beside her. She wondered if he was married. He wasn't wearing a wedding ring, but then that didn't mean anything. A lot of men didn't wear wedding rings...especially ones who enjoyed flirting with other women. One thing was sure: he was far too good-looking for any woman's peace of mind.

'Why is it falling to you to pick up your niece from school?' he asked inquisitively once she had hung up. 'Where are her parents?'

'They are both dead,' Carrie murmured. 'Her mother died two years ago and her father...my brother died in a car crash a few months ago.'

'I'm sorry.' He shook his head, sympathy in his dark eyes. 'Poor little girl.'

'Yes...' For a moment she couldn't say any more as grief encroached suddenly upon her. Tony had only been her half-brother but they had been close, and one of the things that had attracted her to working in Barcelona was that he'd lived not far away. She still couldn't believe that he was dead...it was like some kind of nightmare. 'But we are managing,' she managed to say huskily.

'I'm sure you are. You strike me as an extremely capable young woman. But it can't be easy.'

'We're fine.' She hastily pulled herself together. 'Usually I have a nanny to help me, but she is off this week and it has made things a little more difficult.' She noticed that the taxi was now turning down the street towards the school. 'Anyway, thank you again for allowing me to share your taxi.' She glanced over towards the meter. 'How much do I owe you?'

'I was going this way anyway—please don't bother with payment,' he said quickly.

Carrie was going to argue but suddenly she looked up and saw Molly standing on the pavement outside the school, holding hands with a woman. Leaning forward with a start, she realised it was the little girl's grandmother, and judging by the thunderous expression on her face she was anything but pleased.

What on earth was she doing here? Carrie wondered frantically. She wasn't due to arrive until tomorrow.

'Something wrong?' Max asked, noticing the sudden pallor of her skin.

'No...it's just Molly's grandmother is here and she looks annoyed—probably because I'm late.'

He leaned forward to glance out. 'You're not that late. There are other children just coming out now.'

'Even five minutes isn't going to please Carmel, judging by a letter she sent me recently. She thinks Molly would be better off with her and her husband because I'm not married and I have a demanding career. They say they will have more time for her.'

'That's as may be, but there are lots of single working mothers. As long as Molly is happy with you, I can't see the problem.'

'No, neither can I. I think she means well. She just wants to do her best for her daughter's child. Hopefully I can reassure her that it's in Molly's best interests to be with me.'

The taxi drew up almost level with the unsmiling woman. Carmel McCormack was plump and in her early sixties; she had white hair tied in a bun and she was wearing a floral summer dress. She looked like a very pleasant woman, except for the irate expression on her face.

'Anyway—' Carrie reached hastily for the door handle '—thanks again for the lift.'

Max watched as she climbed out onto the pavement;

observed how the little girl's face lit up when she saw Carrie, and how she ran joyously to be picked up by her.

As the taxi started to move he suddenly noticed that she had left her mobile phone on the seat. He told the driver to stop the cab and then wound down the window. 'Carrie, you have forgotten your phone,' he called.

She looked around and then walked over to take it from him. 'Thanks.' She smiled. 'My mind is definitely not with it at the moment.'

'That's understandable.' His eyes moved to the little girl who had her arms wrapped tightly around her neck, then to the woman who was looking on so disapprovingly from behind. 'Hope all goes well for you, Carrie...see you later.'

Carrie watched as the taxi moved away from her. What did he mean by 'see you later'? she wondered. She probably would never see him again. They were just passing strangers, and she didn't even know his surname. For some reason a pang of regret stole quietly into her thoughts. He had been so handsome and understanding...and so incredibly easy to talk to. She didn't remember ever opening up to a stranger the way she had to him.

But as she turned to face Molly's grandmother she quickly squashed the emotion. She had enough problems in her life without a man complicating things. She needed all her concentration now for Molly.

'Carrie, you are late picking poor Molly up.' Carmel's voice was sharp.

'Only five minutes, Carmel. It's nice to see you,' she added hastily. 'I didn't expect you until tomorrow.'

'I managed to get an earlier flight. My husband will follow tomorrow.'

Carrie nodded and wondered suddenly if the woman had turned up earlier in the hope of catching her out. 'How is Bob?' she asked politely, remembering that Tony had told her his father-in-law had suffered a heart attack earlier in the year.

'He hasn't been at all well.' For a second the angry lines on the woman's face softened. 'Otherwise I would have been here sooner.'

'I'm sorry, Carmel. It must be a difficult time for you,' Carrie said softly.

'It hasn't been easy,' Carmel admitted with a sigh. 'I felt bad about not getting here for Tony's funeral...and I'm worried sick about Molly, the poor little soul.'

Carrie looked down at the child in her arms and cuddled her even closer. 'You're doing fine, aren't you, Mol?' The little girl nodded and then struggled to get down as she saw one of her friends.

'I meant what I said in my letter, Carrie,' the other woman said without hesitation. 'I don't think that you adopting her is a good idea.'

Carrie felt a dart of fear at the brisk certainty in the other woman's voice. 'I don't think we should talk about this now, Carmel. But I have to say, I don't understand your objections.'

'Well, they are quite clear-cut. My granddaughter needs a stable home life, and I'm not so sure that is with a single girl who jets off around the world at the drop of a hat.'

'I don't jet off at the drop of a hat, Carmel,' Carrie said gently. 'I just do my job and then I'm back to take care of her. I also employ a perfectly good nanny to help.'

Other mothers were passing them on the pavement, looking curiously in their direction, and, conscious of the fact that this was not the place for such a discussion, plus worrying that Molly might understand what they were saying, Carrie moved forward. 'Come back to my apartment. I'll make us tea and we can talk in comfort. This isn't for Molly's ears.'

'I think it's best she comes back with me to Australia,'

Carmel continued as if Carrie hadn't spoken. 'I've given it a lot of thought and I know you mean well. But your life is too precarious.'

'Precarious?' Carrie frowned. Obviously Carmel was just overwrought with anxiety, first over her husband and now over her grandchild. 'Really, Carmel, you are quite wrong,' she said gently.

'So who was that man in the taxi with you?' Carmel asked.

'The man…?' Carrie hesitated, thrown by the sudden question. Saying he was some stranger she had just met on the plane didn't sound too good.

'Some boyfriend, I suppose.'

'Well, yes…' Placed on the spot, Carrie thought it seemed the most prudent explanation.

But Carmel didn't look reassured. 'You see, this is just what I'm worried about. I don't think Molly should be subjected to a series of different men in her life. She's just lost her father; she needs constancy.'

'And she will have constancy,' Carrie said, desperately anxious to reassure the woman. 'My relationship with…Max is very settled.'

'Really?' Carmel stopped and suddenly for the first time seemed to be interested. 'You mean you might get married?'

'Well…' Carrie paused; she could sense that a lot was riding on her answer. 'Well, yes, I might,' she murmured. It wasn't exactly a lie; after all, she might get married one day…to somebody.

'Oh, my dear girl!' Carmel put a hand on her chest and seemed overwhelmed with relief. 'I can't tell you how pleased I am to hear that. It puts a whole different complexion on things.'

'Does it?' Carrie bit down on her lip anxiously.

'Well, of course.' Carmel moved and linked her arm

through hers. 'You're right, this isn't the place to discuss things. Let's go back to your apartment.'

'It's just a few minutes' walk around the corner. I'm in a very handy location for work and for Molly's school.' Desperately Carrie tried to steer the conversation onto settled ground as they walked away from the school gates.

'Never mind all that,' Carmel said. 'You must tell me all about your young man. What does he do for a living?'

'He's a lawyer,' Carrie said weakly. She had the horrible feeling that her little white lie was turning into an enormous black hole.

'A lawyer! How wonderful...and he's so handsome. I can't wait to meet him properly. You must bring him to dinner at our hotel tomorrow evening.'

'Oh, I can't!' Carrie was horrified now. 'He's...away on business tomorrow.'

Carmel halted in her tracks. 'But, my dear, it's imperative that we meet him properly.'

'Yes, of course.' Carrie was feeling slightly sick inside. 'I'll see what I can arrange.'

CHAPTER TWO

THE phone on Carrie's desk rang just as she was about to leave the office. 'Carrie Michaels,' she said briskly.

'Hi, Carrie, it's Carmel. I just wondered if you've had a chance to speak to your young man yet? My husband will be arriving tonight, and as it's Saturday tomorrow I thought we could all meet up. I'd like to book a table for lunch at our hotel.'

Carrie felt her heart start to slide down into her stomach. She had been up until midnight last night, trying to reassure Carmel that everything was wonderful in her life. But Carmel had only been interested in one thing—Max. Carrie had tried all sorts of tactics to get her away from the subject but it had kept coming back. So much so that by the time the woman had left to go back to her hotel Carrie had almost been starting to believe in her fake fiancé herself.

And now she was in a situation that was a total mess. Carmel was refusing to be fobbed off with excuses of how busy Max was. So what could she do? It wasn't as if she could conjure Max up out of thin air...

'That sounds a lovely idea, Carmel,' she said gently. 'But I think it will just be Molly and I who join you for lunch. Max is in the middle of a very serious court case. He's not able to get away.'

'Did you tell him that my husband and I are probably only going to be here for a couple of weeks?'

'Yes, and he feels terrible—'

'Well, we'll just have to extend our stay. I had only

booked a one-way ticket anyway,' Carmel said, 'because I was thinking Molly would come back with us.'

The very suggestion made Carrie's blood pressure soar. 'Listen, I've got to go, Carmel, I'm very busy. I'll ring you later.'

What a mess, she thought as she put the phone down. She should never have lied…it was mad…what on earth had possessed her? She was usually such an honest person, and now the one most important thing in her life—keeping Molly—hung in the balance.

'Everything all right, Carrie?' Her boss's voice from the open doorway caught her by surprise.

'Yes, fine,' she lied airily. José was a good-looking man in his late thirties. Like Max, he was Spanish and dark-haired. For a second she found herself looking at him in a whole new way, wondering if he would pass for Max. But as soon as the idea crossed her mind she cancelled it. She really must be desperate. José was her boss and he would not be impressed with the subterfuge. But, more than that, they had started to date at the beginning of the year; it had just been a casual thing, drinks after work and trips to the theatre. She hadn't thought too seriously about it until Molly had come onto the scene. José's objection to her niece had taken her very much by surprise. He had been less than pleased with the intrusion into their well-ordered adult lives. And when she had told him she was going to adopt Molly he had looked horrified. Carrie had immediately cooled things between them, and since then their relationship was back to strictly business.

She should never have mixed business with pleasure in the first place, she told herself crossly now.

'You look a bit tired,' José said. 'Children are hard work, aren't they?'

Carrie noticed the jibe. Not as hard work as dealing with the adults around her at the moment, she thought distractedly. 'Molly is no trouble at all,' she answered firmly. 'I'm just on my way up to the Santos vineyard,' she added, changing the subject firmly back to work.

'Do you think Pablo should go instead?' José asked suddenly.

'Why?' Carrie frowned. 'This is my pitch, José.' She noticed that he had the grace to look a bit embarrassed.

'I know it is. It's just that Pablo said you looked a bit distracted and tired and he kindly offered to step in for you. It's a long drive out to that vineyard.'

I just bet he offered, Carrie thought furiously. The vultures were circling for her job already, and obviously José was allowing them to swoop as another veiled attempt to make her rethink about Molly. But Carrie had no intention of rethinking about Molly. She was more than capable of dealing with her niece and her job.

'The contract is in the bag, José,' she said, picking up her briefcase. 'And it will be signed and sealed either today or very early next week.'

José looked suitably impressed.

As well he might be, Carrie thought as she headed out to the car park. She had to get this contract now; it was a matter of professional pride.

She used the drive to the Santos vineyard to go over the facts and figures in her head.

The estate was very impressive, she thought as she turned into the driveway after the long journey. Vast fields stretched for as far as the eye could see, laid out in long, regimented rows of vines. Then at last she turned a corner and the main house came into sight. It was built in the Spanish style, with round arches and circular bays, and it glistened white in the sun against a hazy backdrop of purple mountains.

Although it was obviously the home of a wealthy man it had all the charm and rustic style of a country retreat.

Carrie fell instantly in love with the place; she adored the scarlet geraniums that spilled from terracotta pots on the terraces and the purple bougainvillea that climbed around windows with dark green shutters open to the heat of the day.

The gardens that surrounded the villa made it look like a bejewelled oasis; there were palm trees and tropical flowers and the grass was so green it looked like velvet.

She pulled her car to a halt by the front entrance and stepped out. Immediately the intense heat of the afternoon hit her. The air was still and silent except for the sound of the sprinkling system and the sizzling sound of parched earth lapping up the moisture.

The front door opened and a stocky man of medium build came out. He was in his mid-thirties, Carrie guessed. 'Miss Michaels, I'm Manuel Barrera, Estate Manager of Santos Wines.'

'Pleased to meet you, Señor Barrera.' She had been speaking on the phone to this man for the past few weeks, and he seemed very pleasant. She just hoped she could keep him on side so he would sign the go-ahead for their campaign. 'And please call me Carrie.'

She looked up as someone else came through the front door and felt a deep jolt of shock as her eyes met with the dark intense gaze of her fake fiancé Max.

'Please allow me to present Max Santos,' Manuel said with a flourish. 'The managing director of Santos Wines.'

'We've already met.' Carrie's voice was cool. She didn't like being made a fool of, and she thought it highly disingenuous that this man had sat next to her listening to her ideas about his company without informing her he had a vested interest. What kind of game was he playing? she wondered angrily. And he'd lied to her, told her he was a lawyer.

Max watched the expression of shock and then annoyance on her face with a gleam of amusement in his eyes. 'Good to see you again, Carrie.'

Quickly she composed herself and forced herself to smile back at him with cool reserve. She needed this contract; if she botched it up her rivals in the office would be rubbing their hands with glee. 'Max. This is a surprise!'

He smiled as if her amiable tone amused him greatly. 'A pleasant one, I hope. Manuel is going to give you the grand tour of the vineyard and then afterwards perhaps you'd like to stay and we can discuss business over some lunch?'

'Thank you, that would be nice.' Her voice was stiffly polite.

Carrie hoped that he was going to disappear after that and leave her with Manuel. At least that way she would have a chance to gather her senses and think about this situation. But to her dismay he accompanied them as they turned towards a courtyard at the side of the house.

Every now and then she darted a glance over at him. He was dressed more casually today in lightweight beige trousers and a matching open-necked shirt. If anything the informal attire made him appear even more handsome, but it wasn't just his looks that kept drawing her eyes—it was his air of latent power. There was a strength about him that gave him a raw sensuality that was magnetising.

'How is your niece today, Carrie?' he asked as he stepped back to allow her to precede him into vast, cavernous cellars.

'She's fine, thank you.'

'Her grandmother wasn't angry with you for long?'

'No, not long.' For a second Carrie wondered what he would say if she told him about the lie she had made up about him. He'd probably be horrified. He was probably married with six children.

Carrie tried to concentrate her attention on the enormous wooden vats that lined the walls. 'You've got a very impressive place here,' she said, desperately trying to concentrate on work.

The estate manager started to tell her about the process of wine making that they used. And she tried very hard to give him her complete attention. But all the time she was acutely conscious of Max's watchful eyes on her.

What was his game? she wondered. Why had he not told her who he was yesterday? Was he just stringing her along before telling her that in actual fact he wouldn't be requiring her advertising services? Surely if he was really interested in her ideas he would have told her so on the plane yesterday and then introduced himself?

As Manuel paused to lead the way through into the next cellar Carrie pulled together the presence of mind to ask some pertinent questions, but all the while she was conscious of the fact that Max was taking in her every move, her every word. For a moment she found herself wishing she had worn something more attractive today. Her dark blue business suit was smart but there was nothing alluring about it...

Not that she wanted to attract him, of course. This was purely business.

As they stepped back outside into the blinding glare of the sunshine Carrie missed her step and Max reached quickly to catch hold of her arm. For an instant she was held close beside him. And in that moment she wondered what it would be like to make love with him, to have those strong hands caress her naked body...

The thought made desire race through her body like molten lava.

'Are you okay?' he asked gently.

'Yes...thank you.' She moved away from him abruptly, horrified by the direction her thoughts had taken. She knew nothing about the man…They walked down into the vineyard. After the cool of the cellars the heat of the sun felt even more intense, but maybe that was partly due to the thoughts that had been racing around in her mind, Carrie thought wryly.

A member of staff came to talk to Manuel and Carrie found herself alone with Max. She glanced over at him uncertainly, feeling unaccountably shy.

'Why didn't you tell me who you were when we were talking on the plane yesterday?'

He shrugged, not in the slightest bit perturbed by the question. 'I thought it might have influenced what you had to say.'

'Well, of course it would.' Her blue eyes snapped with sudden fire. 'You had an unfair advantage over me!'

'Maybe I did.' He smiled. 'And I enjoyed it.'

There was a husky undertone to his voice that made her blood race. Resolutely she tried to ignore the effect he was having on her. 'This isn't a game, you know. This contract is important to me.'

'I know, I saw that for myself yesterday.'

'But you still didn't tell me who you were,' she persisted, her eyes narrowed. 'And that stunt you played, ordering Santos wine on the plane and asking for my opinion… I suppose if I had said I didn't like it I wouldn't be standing here now. I'd have just been told on the phone this morning that my services were not required.'

'I would never have said that to you.' Max said the words in a low undertone, a flicker of teasing warmth in his dark eyes now. 'I can assure you I would still have invited you up here to have lunch with me, no matter what your opinion of the Santos wine.'

Carrie wasn't quite sure how to take that. Was she imagining the personal undercurrent to the words or did he simply mean that he would still have done business with her? She looked away from him and fell silent. It was strange how easily he could disconcert her. She was normally a confident person, especially in her business affairs. Yet around him she felt totally out of her depth.

Desperately she tried to think of something to say that would take the conversation back strictly to business. But nothing came to mind.

She noticed that the grapes were full and ripe on the vines, their skins gleaming a deep, luscious purple. 'So when will you be harvesting the grapes?' she asked lightly. 'They look very good—in fact good enough to eat.'

'They are. We'll be starting to pick them soon.' He reached out and took one off the vine. 'Would you like to try one?'

She nodded and thought that he would hand it to her; instead he reached closer and placed the grape against her lips in a feather-light caress. There was something so intensely erotic and personal about the move that Carrie felt her skin flush with vivid colour.

'So what do you think?' Max asked, a small smile curving his lips.

'It's…it's very good.' She couldn't quite bring herself to meet his eyes. She didn't know if it was her imagination but there seemed to be an atmosphere between them that felt taut with sensuality.

Manuel came back to join them. 'Sorry about that,' he said politely. 'There's a problem with delivery dates, Max. I'm afraid I'm going to have to go up to the office to sort it out.'

'We're finished here anyway,' Max said easily.

'When you have time I'd like a word with you later,' Manuel said. 'It is urgent, so could we speak after lunch?'

Max nodded. 'Come on up to the house when you are ready.'

With a wave in Carrie's direction, Manuel strode off back in the direction they had just come from.

'Sorry about that. Things are pretty hectic around here at the moment,' Max said. 'Let's go up to the house.' He put a hand at her back to steer her in the right direction. The touch against her body was light yet Carrie imagined she could feel it burning through the delicate material of her dress.

There was a part of her that wanted to move closer towards him…and another part that wanted to run away from the dangerous undercurrents rushing between them. He was probably married with children, she reminded herself again sharply.

That stunt he had pulled yesterday proved he liked to play his cards close to his chest. So she needed to tread warily and keep her wits about her.

Opening the front door, he stood back to allow her to enter the house before him. He had impeccable manners, she noted. It was something she liked in a man. Forcefully she tried to steer her mind away from the things she liked about Max. He was obviously a shrewd businessman and that was all that should concern her.

Carrie glanced around the entrance hall to the villa. She liked the cool marble floors and the majestic staircase that curved gracefully down with a most magnificent wrought-iron banister. There were a few doors leading off in various directions, but Max led her through the nearest one and into a lounge that was light and airy. It had the same marble floors as the hallway. Large white settees with pale blue striped cushions echoed the blue of a swimming pool that lapped outside on the white terrazzo terrace.

The interior design of the property was fabulous and everywhere there were vases of fresh flowers. She found herself gearing herself up to meet his wife. He had to be married...this place was too perfect and he was too handsome.

'Shall we sit outside on the terrace?' Max asked as he opened the patio doors and led the way outside to a table and chairs strategically placed to look out over the garden towards the mountains.

'It's beautiful here.' Carrie didn't sit down immediately. She leaned against the balustrade, her eyes following a grassy path that led down towards an orange grove.

'Yes, I like it.' As Max spoke his eyes didn't move from her face.

She was aware of him watching her and it made her acutely self-conscious. Why was he looking at her like that? she wondered.

'Do you live here alone?' she asked, and hoped the question didn't sound as if she were too interested.

'Yes, I do.'

'Really?' She was surprised, and it showed clearly in her eyes now as she looked over at him.

'Yes, really.' He grinned as if he found her reaction extremely amusing. 'I had this house built a few years ago. Other members of my family live nearby, and my parents live in the main family house in the other direction, about ten kilometres.'

'This is a big place for one person,' she said hurriedly, trying to cover her incredulity.

'I suppose it is. But I like my space.'

'Yes, I do too. But I've always been happy with my apartment up until now,' she found herself telling him impulsively. 'It's compact and central and was the answer to all my requirements when I purchased it. But since Molly has come into my life I want to look for something with a bit more space myself.' She smiled at him. 'Nothing as grand as this, of course, just a little place with a manageable garden where she can play.' She paused for a moment. 'That's providing I get custody, of course.'

He noticed the sudden shadow that crossed her blue eyes. 'Molly means a lot to you, doesn't she?' he said softly.

'Yes.' Carrie raised her chin and met his eyes squarely. 'She means absolutely everything; she is the only family I have left.'

'I can understand that. Family is very important. For instance this estate has been passed down from father to son for generations. As I'm the only son it will all be my responsibility one day, until I pass it on to my children.'

'That feeling of continuity must be very rewarding,' Carrie murmured.

'In some ways.' He shrugged. 'In other ways it can be a pressure.'

'What kind of a pressure?' she asked curiously.

Max hesitated for a moment. 'Well…nearly all my family work in the wine business, my uncles and cousins… So it is extremely important that its success is maintained.'

'Well, I can take one weight off your mind,' Carrie said promptly. 'When you employ *Images* advertising services you won't be making a mistake.'

Max laughed. 'You're a shrewd businesswoman, do you know that?'

'Of course.' She nodded. 'Which is why you should employ my services for your vineyard.'

A young Spanish woman came out onto the terrace behind them and interrupted to ask in halting English if they would like a drink before lunch.

'A glass of lemonade would be nice,' Carrie said as Max looked enquiringly over at her.

'Still keeping a clear head for business?' he asked with a grin as they were left alone again.

'I don't drink much,' she said with a shrug. 'Which is the real reason I hadn't got around to tasting your wine before yesterday.'

She looked over at him and met his eyes and there was silence between them for a moment. 'Why did you tell me yesterday that you're a lawyer?' she asked him huskily, needing to know the truth.

'Because I am.'

She frowned. 'But I thought you ran this place?'

'I am on the board of directors but I haven't taken on the full responsibility for the vineyards yet. That won't happen until my father decides to retire.'

'Oh, I see.'

'Unfortunately my father is in hospital at the moment. He had a mild stroke a few weeks ago. Which means I've had to take time out from my own work to step into his shoes for a while.'

'I'm so sorry. How is your father?'

'He's fine. The doctors say he will make a complete recovery.'

'At least that is a relief for you.'

Max nodded. 'Yes, it is. But it's been a shock. I thought my father was invincible... I thought I'd have a lot more time being independent from the Santos empire. Now I'm not so sure.'

Their drinks arrived and Max led the way over to the table and pulled out one of the chairs for her. Then he leaned back in his chair and surveyed her steadily.

'Anyway, that's enough about that boring subject—tell me about you.'

'I told you about me yesterday,' she said with a rueful smile. 'In fact, I think I told you far too much. Probably bored you to tears.'

'I can assure you that wasn't the case,' Max said with a small smile.

Something about his smile pulled at her heartstrings. Hastily she looked away. Max was a charmer, and she knew the dangers of falling for one of them. 'Anyway, I suppose we should get down to business. What did you think about my ideas yesterday?'

'I thought they were good,' he said truthfully. 'My father would approve.'

'Will you have to run these ideas past him? Or will you have the final say?'

'I'm trying to keep all business decisions away from my father at the moment,' Max said briskly. 'As his health isn't good my mother doesn't want him bothered by any kind of decision-making. So I will have the final say.' He grinned wryly. 'There, you've dragged it out of me. But that doesn't mean I'll be signing on the dotted line without going over everything in minute detail again.'

'I can live with that,' she said, feeling pleased with herself for even pinning him down that much.

'Even if it means staying for an extra-long lunch?' he asked with a smile.

'Absolutely.' She smiled back. 'My time is yours.'

'Now, that is encouraging.'

Carrie looked into his eyes and for a moment she felt as if some invisible magnetising force were pulling her towards him. She wondered suddenly what he would say if she asked him to come to lunch tomorrow to meet Molly's grandmother and pretend to be her partner. As soon as the idea crossed her mind she discarded it in horror. She knew from experience the dangers of mixing business with her personal life. It was a golden rule she intended to stick to from now on. And anyway Max Santos would probably be appalled if she told him of her little white lie...might even decide to take his advertising contract elsewhere; he was a businessman, after all, and he'd want someone who could give one hundred per cent to his advertising, not someone with personal problems.

'Anyway...' Hastily she looked away from him and reached for her briefcase. 'Let's see now...I do have some more details that I need to discuss.'

Max watched the way she calmly opened her leather briefcase. He admired her professionalism, and she intrigued him...it had been a long time since a woman had done that.

Carrie riffled through the pages hurriedly until she found the relevant details.

For a while their conversation centred on the papers in front of her, but it took all of Carrie's resolve to remain focused. She was aware of everything about him: his smile made her heat up inside—even his businesslike questions seemed to stir excitement inside her.

She was relieved when the housekeeper arrived to tell them that lunch was served, giving her a few moments to gather her senses.

Max led her through to a dining room that also opened up onto the terrace. What was it about this man that made her feel like this? she wondered suddenly as she took a seat opposite him at a long, polished table and watched as he poured her a glass of wine. Why did she sense danger every time her eyes collided with his?

'So, if you are happy with my suggestions, perhaps we could finalise the details and close our deal today?' she suggested briskly.

'You seem to be in quite a hurry suddenly, Carrie,' he remarked.

'Well, you know what they say, time is money.' She met his eyes directly for a moment. 'But then I sense that you don't like to waste time either.'

He smiled at that. 'You're right, I don't. But I've still got time for our extra-long lunch.'

'Yes, of course.' She laughed, and then, unable to hold his gaze for any longer, she looked away. 'But I dare not be too late back to Barcelona today otherwise Molly's grandmother will have me hung.' Deliberately she lightened her tone and concentrated her attention on the salad appetiser of mozzarella cheese and vine tomatoes that the housekeeper placed before her. It was drizzled with olive oil and garnished with fresh basil, giving it the healthy, succulent taste of the Mediterranean.

Max watched her closely across the table. He had never met a woman who tried to keep herself so reserved, so aloof. He sensed that she used her work as a barrier to hide behind—that for all those sharp, businesslike responses she was extremely vulnerable. He wondered suddenly if she had been badly hurt by somebody in the past.

'Well, I'll try not to keep you too late,' he said softly. 'Are you picking Molly up from school?'

'No, her grandma has asked to do that. She wants to spend some time with her.'

'Then I presume you are hurrying back for some hot date?'

'Certainly not. I have enough complications in my life at the moment! I simply want to be back at my apartment when Carmel arrives with Molly. We have a lot to discuss.'

'Between that and work, life seems pretty hectic for you,' he said nonchalantly. 'I'm the same, running between this place and my work.'

They were interrupted by a sudden commotion out in the hallway. Carrie looked around and saw that it was Manuel, arriving accompanied by two boisterous children, a boy and girl of about Molly's age. They looked like twins.

'Sorry about this disruption,' Manuel said from the open doorway. 'They've been sent home on a half-day from school and my wife has been delayed in town. I'm just going to go and drop them with their grandma.'

'That's okay,' Max said easily. He didn't seem fazed as the children caught sight of him and hurried through the doorway to greet him.

Carrie watched as he pushed his chair back from the table and welcomed them both with a bear-like hug, ruffling their hair and grinning as they chatted to him excitedly.

They were attractive children with dark hair and eyes very like their father, and they were talking in rapid Spanish. 'Uncle Max, Mum says we can have a birthday party in our back garden next week and that you'll come and so will everyone else and we might have pony rides and a barbecue—'

'Hey, you two, steady on,' Manuel said laughingly from the doorway. 'Uncle Max is in the middle of a business meeting. He doesn't want to hear about your birthday party.'

'On the contrary, I'm very interested,' Max said with a grin.

Carrie watched as the children perched one on each knee, and she found herself comparing Max's easy manner with the awkward way José had behaved around Molly. If Molly had interrupted like this, José would have been totally irritated; he'd had no patience or time for Molly at all.

'Carrie, these are Manuel's children,' Max introduced her cheerfully. 'Belle and Emilio. It will be their fifth birthday a week on Sunday.'

'Hello, you two.' Carrie smiled and spoke to them in Spanish. 'It sounds like you will be having a great party.'

They launched into an excited and noisy description of their party plans and Carrie found herself laughing and asking them more questions.

'I just came over to tell you that your father rang through to the office a little while ago, asking about these delivery dates,' Manuel said to Max. 'I told him everything was under control, but he seemed to be fretting about things.'

Max shook his head. 'I'll pop down to the hospital a little later and reassure him. All he should be thinking about is getting well.'

'Yes, that's exactly what I told him,' Manuel agreed, 'but you know what he's like. Doesn't like to listen.'

The housekeeper brought in their main courses.

'Come on, children, we need to go and leave Uncle Max and Carrie in peace.'

The twins seemed reluctant to move, especially when Max started to tickle them unmercifully and make them giggle.

He was good with children, Carrie thought idly. And she thought suddenly that maybe she had misjudged him yesterday when she had thought he was just a flirtatious Casanova type like her ex-husband...she didn't even know him.

As the twins slipped down off his knee they grinned over at Carrie. 'Are you Uncle Max's new girlfriend?' the little girl asked her suddenly.

Before Carrie or Max could answer that question their father was shooing them out of the room, sending profuse apologies in Carrie's direction. 'Sorry about this; see you later, Max. Perhaps we can have that talk before you go down to the hospital?'

'Yes, give me an hour, Manuel, and then come up.'

As the front door closed behind them Max grinned over at Carrie. 'Having kids around is a bit like having a whirling dervish rushing through the house, isn't it?'

'Yes, but the funny thing is that as soon as they have gone and peace reigns supreme, you find yourself thinking it's too quiet.' She smiled. 'Strange thing is that I used to think I enjoyed my solitary life…pleasing myself…going out when I wanted. But I wouldn't change what I've got with Molly for all the treasures in the world.'

Max smiled. 'Well, hopefully you won't have to.'

'No…hopefully.' Carrie fell silent as she helped herself to some paella made with tiger prawns and smoked fish.

Max lifted the wine bottle. 'Would you like another glass?' he offered politely.

She shook her head. 'No, I have to drive back, plus I need my wits about me when dealing with Molly's grandmother. Carmel is quite a formidable character.'

'Yes, I suppose we both need to keep a clear head, Carrie. Seeing as I'm going back to the hospital to try persuade my father to forget about the business and that I have it all in hand.'

'He doesn't want to let go of the reins, I take it?' Carrie asked.

'Well, it's a similar situation to yours with Molly's grandmother. If I told him I was settling down and getting married he'd feel a lot happier leaving things in my hands. But as it is he thinks I jet off too much with my job and that the vineyard needs more full-time attention.'

'And does it need full-time attention?'

'At the moment I'm afraid it does…with my father's health being bad things have slipped a bit recently. Plus we have an added predicament that Manuel is leaving to set up his own business. He has been the cornerstone of the Santos vineyard for a long time and I think he feels bad that he is leaving now when my father is so ill, especially as he is part of the family. But he has been offered a wonderful opportunity and I've told him he should take it.'

'So who will take over the running of the vineyard here?'

'Well, if I know my father, he is going to insist on going back to work as soon as he can,' Max said, his voice grave. 'I'd suggest getting in another manager, but I can't see him being happy with that. Unfortunately he is a stubborn traditionalist and he's not going to be happy retiring until I take over full time. Preferably with a wife at my side.'

'I'm surprised you aren't married,' she said nonchalantly. 'You seem very good with children.'

'Hey, don't you start.' He grinned. 'I have enough of those kind of statements from my parents. But for the record I very nearly did tie the knot a few years ago. What about you?' he asked suddenly.

'I was married when I was in my early twenties but it was a mistake; we were divorced three years later.' Carrie's lips twisted wryly.

Watching her closely, Max wondered if that accounted for that wariness he saw in her deep blue eyes on occasions. 'And you've never considered taking the plunge again?'

Carrie shook her head. 'That's too much of a lottery for my tastes. I like my life exactly the way it is. It's orderly and uncomplicated and I feel as if I'm in control, which makes me happy...' She trailed off, wondering why she had just told him that. It was far too personal.

'So, apart from Molly, you are a true career girl.'

'Yes, I suppose I am.'

'I can relate to that,' Max answered with slow deliberation. 'Like you, I enjoy being in control of my own destiny. That's why I decided to carve out my own business instead of staying here in the family firm. Obviously my father wasn't too happy about my decision at the time, but I think he realises now that it was something I just needed to do to prove I could be successful in my own right.'

'And what will you do now that the vineyard is in crisis?' she asked curiously. 'Will you give your work up and take over the reins full time here?'

'Yes. If my father refuses to retire I will. Ultimately this vineyard is my home, the place I was born to be. That sense of belonging is a very strong pull.'

Something about the way he said that struck a chord inside Carrie. She had never had that sense of belonging. Her mother had died when she was seven and she had been sent to live with her father and stepmother. She had never felt she belonged in her father's new life. The only good thing that had come out of it had been her half-brother Tony…and his daughter Molly.

Swiftly she tried to focus away from Tony before her grief started to encroach. There was no use looking back; the future and Molly were all that mattered. And she was going to have to go back and face Molly's grandmother with determination, tell her the truth: that there was no man in her life but that she was self-sufficient and more than capable of giving Molly a good home.

The housekeeper came back in to ask if they had any further requirements.

Carrie straightened her cutlery on the plate. 'No, that was absolutely delicious, thank you very much,' she said.

Carrie glanced at her watch as the dishes were removed from the table and was surprised to find she had been here over three hours. 'Heavens, I'd better make a move,' she said swiftly. 'I didn't realise it was so late.' She reached for her case and brought out a copy of the advertising contract. 'I'll leave this for you to look over, Max,' she said. 'If you are happy with the contents you could sign it and post it back to me tomorrow.'

Max didn't reply immediately. 'Perhaps I could return it in person tomorrow evening? It's Saturday night—we could have dinner together.'

The softly asked question sent shivers of awareness through her. 'That's not really necessary, Max,' she said swiftly.

'Maybe not necessary, but pleasurable,' he murmured confidently.

Was he flirting with her? she wondered suddenly, alarm bells ringing. Here was a man used to women agreeing with his every word, but that wasn't her style...and this was business. 'If you would like to come into the office on Monday morning to discuss any changes you'd like to make, then that's fine,' she said quickly. 'But I'm busy tomorrow night.'

Max accepted her reply with nonchalant indifference. 'I'll phone you on Monday and we will arrange something then. How's that?'

'Yes...' Carrie pushed her chair back from the table. 'Yes, that's fine.'

Max watched as she opened her bag and took out a business card. 'My office number,' she said swiftly, handing it across to him. 'Remember nothing is set in stone— we can change things to suit your requirements.'

'Good, I like a bit of flexibility.' He grinned at her and it made her heart skip in a crazy way inside her chest.

'Right, well, I should go now. She felt it imperative to get out of here fast, before she found herself agreeing to have dinner with him. It would be so easy just to say yes. Business and pleasure don't mix, she told herself again firmly.

'So I'll speak to you on Monday,' she said briskly as they stepped outside into the sunshine.

'You will indeed.' She wondered if it was her imagination, or was his tone huskily deep with an undertone of promise?

To counteract the feeling she tried to be even more businesslike. 'Thank you for your time.' As they reached her car she turned and held out her hand to end the meeting in a formal way.

But as he reached to shake her hand there was nothing conventional about the feelings that suddenly raced through her body. The touch of his skin against hers was electric.

Hurriedly she pulled away from him and got into her car; her heart was bouncing against her ribs. The last man who'd had this effect on her was her ex-husband. The lessons learnt there were too strong to ignore. Max Santos had to be strictly kept at arm's length, she told herself fiercely as she turned the key in the engine.

'Bye, now.' She gave him a half-wave as the car moved forward.

He smiled. 'Until next week.'

As Max stood and watched her drive away he wondered whom she was seeing tomorrow night for dinner. Was it business or pleasure? He found himself hoping it was the former…he wanted to see much more of Carrie Michaels. He sensed a challenge there and that interested him greatly.

CHAPTER THREE

MOLLY had got hold of Carrie's lipstick and trailed it everywhere; red was smeared over her cute heart-shaped face and over her sweet cupid lips in a swirling sea of colour.

'Hey, you, what have you been doing?' Carrie asked playfully as she emerged from her *en suite* bathroom and saw the little girl sitting at the dressing table going through her make-up bag.

Molly chuckled happily and dived back into the bag to take out some blusher, putting it on her cheeks in big dabs that made her look like a clown.

'I know we are going out for lunch, and you want to look good for Grandma and Grandpa, but I don't think they will appreciate the make-up, darling,' Carrie said, taking the brush away from the little girl.

She picked the child up and brought her into the bathroom to shower her. Molly giggled with pleasure as Carrie teased her and tickled her. It was amazing how a child could lift your spirits, Carrie thought. She was dreading this meeting with Carmel and her husband because she was going to have to own up to the fact that she was on her own, that there was no wonderful fiancé. She had been trying to gather up the courage to tell Carmel this since coming back from the Santos vineyard yesterday, but the truth kept sticking in Carrie's throat. Maybe with Molly's grandfather there it would be easier, she told herself now. Because the whole thing was ridiculous; she was more than capable of giving her niece a good home life all on her own.

Taking Molly out of the shower, she brought her back to the bedroom. 'What shall we wear for lunch with Grandma?' she asked the little girl as she opened the wardrobe and raked through the contents. 'How about your pink dress?' She took the garment out and examined it carefully. It was an outfit she had bought for Molly when she had been on a business trip to the Paris office a few months before Tony had died; she remembered ringing him from the store and asking his opinion about the size.

'Get the bigger size,' he had said immediately. 'She's growing up so fast, it's quite scary. I'll be walking her down the aisle before we know it.'

The memory made Carrie's eyes blur with sudden tears. Hurriedly she blinked them back. She needed to be in complete control this afternoon; there was no time for grief.

Towel-drying Molly's black curls, she then sat her at the dressing table and brushed them neatly into place before pulling the pink dress over her head. The effect was perfect; she looked like a little princess, her hair shining and her large eyes dominating the small face.

'Can I take Mojo with me?' Molly asked, picking up the white rag dog that she liked to take everywhere she went.

'Of course you can,' Carrie said quickly.

'Will Daddy be at the hotel?' the little girl asked suddenly.

The question made Carrie's heart catch. She had tried to explain to Molly about her father's death, and the little girl had seemed to understand, but every now and then she still asked for him. How did you explain to a child who was only just four that Daddy was never coming back? Carrie wondered, drawing the child up and into her arms and holding her tight. 'No, darling, do you remember what I told you about Daddy?'

Molly pulled away from her and nodded. 'He's in heaven,' she said solemnly.

'But he still loves you very much and so do Grandma and Grandpa, and they are looking forward to seeing you. Grandpa just flew in from Australia on a big plane last night. He's going to tell you all about it. Isn't that exciting?'

Molly nodded and then wriggled to get down out of her arms. 'Can I have ice cream at the hotel?'

'You can have anything you want, darling,' Carrie said softly. The clock in the hall struck twelve and it made Carrie hurry to select her own outfit from the wardrobe. She had thirty minutes to gather herself together and work out what was best to tell Carmel.

Carrie selected a cream trouser suit and a silk camisole for underneath, and then, pinning her hair back from her face, she lightly applied some make-up.

The effect was understated and elegant. She looked confident…even if she didn't feel it, she thought wryly.

Exactly on time Carrie's taxi pulled up outside the Grand Hotel, which stood on one of Barcelona's main thoroughfares. The entrance was extremely imposing and a doorman in red and white livery came and opened the door of her taxi for her. She took Molly's hand and they went in through the swing doors. It was cool inside, a welcome relief from the humid heat of the day.

Carrie had been here a few times in the past, usually on business lunches to seal important deals, yet never had she felt as nervous as she did today. She walked across the marble entrance hall to the long reception desk and was just about to ask for someone to ring upstairs to Carmel's room when she spotted a familiar figure coming in the other direction across the foyer.

Her heart started its familiar speed-racing as she saw it was Max Santos. He looked fabulously attractive in a lightweight grey suit that seemed to give him that air of distinguished authority that made Carrie go weak inside.

He caught sight of her at the same time and smiled warmly. 'Hello, Carrie, this is a surprise.'

'Yes, isn't it?' she said faintly. The last thing she needed was Max lurking around at the same time as Molly's grandparents. 'What are you doing here?'

'I've been meeting with my accountant over coffee.' Max's eyes moved from Carrie to her niece. 'Hello, Molly, it's nice to see you.'

Molly gave him a wide smile and seemed to be quite taken with Max's friendly demeanour. 'I'm going to have ice cream for my lunch,' she told him happily, scuffing her shiny black shoes against the marble floor as she spoke.

'They do some wonderful ice cream here,' Max said seriously. 'Try the raspberry sorbet…it's great.'

Molly nodded and then held out the rag dog in her hands. 'This is Mojo,' she told Max. 'He likes ice cream too.'

'Pleased to meet you, Mojo,' Max said, reaching out to shake the dog's paw. 'I'm Max.'

Carrie found herself smiling at this exchange, for a moment her nerves forgotten.

'I take it you are here to meet Molly's grandparents?' Max asked as he transferred his attention back towards her.

'Yes, they are staying here and they've asked us to have lunch with them.'

Max nodded. 'I'm glad I bumped into you. I have a few details about that contract that I'd like to clear with you.'

'Well, we will have to discuss them on Monday, Max, I'm rather busy.' Over his shoulder she suddenly saw Molly's grandparents coming down the long, sweeping staircase.

'How about dinner tomorrow?' Max asked her resolutely. 'I'm going to be very busy on Monday.'

'Well, perhaps Tuesday morning at the office, then.' As desperate as she was to get rid of Max she didn't want to tie herself down to an evening appointment—not with Molly's grandparents on the scene. She wanted to prove to them that she had plenty of time for their granddaughter, not that she had to meet business clients at all hours.

'This is important, Carrie,' Max said with a firm determination. 'I want to get this advertising contract up and running as soon as possible.'

'Well, I tell you what, ring me tomorrow and we'll organise something. You'll find my mobile number on my business card.' Carrie was desperate to get away from him now; Carmel had reached the bottom of the stairs and had seen them.

'Goodbye, Max.' Fixing a smile on her face, she tried to bypass him and head Carmel off before she noticed to whom she was speaking.

'Look, Molly, darling, here are Grandma and Grandpa,' Carrie said, reaching to take hold of Molly's hand to lead her away. Molly glanced across and then to Carrie's surprise she pulled her hand abruptly away from her. 'I want to go home,' she cried suddenly. 'I want to go home now.'

'But we are going to have ice cream and a lovely time,' Carrie said gently. 'Come on, Molly.' Before Carrie could take hold of her hand again, the child moved speedily away from her and started running across the foyer towards the front door. At the same time a waiter was coming through the dining-room doors with a tray of glasses. The two collided with a bump and two glasses tipped over onto the tiled floor with a resounding crash.

There was a moment's silence as everyone passing through the busy foyer looked around to see what the commotion was. Hurriedly Carrie moved to take charge.

'Are you all right, darling?' She bent to check that no shards of glass had harmed the little girl and at the same time glanced up at the waiter to apologise profusely.

'It's okay, no problem,' the waiter assured her. 'I'll just get someone to clear this glass.'

'You are all right now, Molly,' Carrie soothed reassuringly to the child who looked scared now by what had happened.

'Want to go home,' she wailed.

'You're fine, darling, there is no harm done, and there are no cuts or bruises,' Carrie assured her gently.

'Want to go home.' Molly's voice was louder and her bottom lip wobbled precariously.

Carmel and her husband Bob came to stand beside them. 'Really, Carrie, what were you thinking of, allowing Molly to run wild like that?' Carmel asked in a shocked tone. Her face was red with anxiety and her husband, a tall, thin man with horn-rimmed spectacles, looked equally perturbed.

Molly started to cry. 'Behave yourself, Molly,' Carmel said firmly. 'This is no way to behave.'

'She's fine, Carmel.' Carrie sought to soothe the situation in a gentle tone. 'Aren't you, darling? You just got a bit scared and shy for a minute. That was it, wasn't it?'

Molly just continued to cry.

'It's okay, darling,' Carrie hushed her. 'Everything is

okay. This is your grandma—remember, from yesterday? And Grandpa who has come all the way from Australia. They want to say hello and sit and talk with you.'

'Don't want to…want to go home,' Molly said again, burying her head against Carrie's shoulder.

'Have you put these ideas into her head?' Carmel asked Carrie sharply. 'Bob, say something,' she instructed her husband.

'Come on, young lady.' Bob's voice held a strict authoritarian tone and he held out his hand towards the child. 'That's quite enough of this.'

Molly refused to let go of Carrie's neck, refused to even look around. She was shaking.

They were all taken by surprise as Max stepped in and crouched down beside Carrie. 'This is a lot of fuss about nothing, isn't it?' he said soothingly and reached out to ruffle the top of Molly's curls. 'Look who you have forgotten, Molly.'

Carrie noticed that he was holding the little girl's dog in his hand. 'It's Mojo—he fell on the hard floor and hurt his foot.' He waggled the toy dog next to Molly's cheek and she looked up.

Max made a gruff little noise as if the dog was barking and then cuddled the toy in against her. 'Poor Mojo, better kiss him better,' he said.

Molly pulled away from Carrie and reached for the dog, burying her head against him for a moment.

'There, that's better, isn't it?' Max asked softly. Molly nodded and gave him a crooked smile that was half tearful, half relieved.

Carrie's eyes connected with Max's over the child's head and she also smiled at him gratefully. 'Thank you,' she mouthed softly.

He smiled back, a steady, reassuring kind of smile that

made everything suddenly feel as if it was going to be all right. Then he got to his feet and looked over at Molly's grandparents.

'Molly's behaviour is very understandable,' he said in a voice that was quiet and yet filled with resolute strength. 'She is feeling a little shy and unsure today, that's all. A little reassurance is all she needs.' It was the kind of voice that no one would ever like to argue with.

'Of course.' Carmel was the first to pull herself together. 'I agree entirely. We were just worried, that's all. We want the very best for Molly. Don't we, Bob?'

Her husband nodded. 'Of course we do. This isn't easy for any of us. We want to do our duty by our grandchild.' He extended his hand. 'I guess you are Max Santos, Carrie's fiancé? Carmel has been telling me all about you; you're a lawyer, aren't you?'

Carrie felt her heart dive somewhere into her shoes in total panic. Quickly she lifted Molly and stood up.

'Yes, I'm a lawyer.' Max's voice held a note of puzzlement, which was hardly surprising. But he still shook the other man's hand.

Desperately Carrie tried to think of something to break the conversation, some way of getting Max away from here before things got even more seriously out of control. But before she could say anything, Carmel was interrupting.

'I'm so relieved that you could come today. Carrie was telling us that you are in the middle of an important court case and that you might not be able to meet with us at all.'

Max turned dryly amused dark eyes onto Carrie and she felt herself starting to blush bright red.

Carmel reached across to shake his hand. 'We did see

each other briefly outside school the other day, but you were rushing off to court.'

'That's right.' Max's eyes still hadn't moved from Carrie's face.

'So we are very relieved to meet you today. Did your court case finish earlier than you had expected?'

'Actually, Carmel, Max can't stay. He is rushing off back to work,' Carrie interjected hurriedly. 'You were just dropping us off, weren't you, Max?' Carrie's blue eyes beseeched him to just agree and then disappear. She would have to make her apologies and explanations to him later.

For a second he hesitated and then he smiled. 'No, on the contrary. I have time to stay and have some lunch.'

The words caused a deep jolt of shock inside Carrie. What was going on here? she wondered.

'But if you don't mind we won't stay long, Carmel,' Max continued smoothly. 'I think Molly needs the famili- arity of Carrie's apartment, with her own toys and books and just a little TLC from her aunt.'

'Fine, we will go through to the dining room.' Carmel and Bob turned to lead the way. And as they turned their backs Carrie put a detaining hand on Max's shoulder. 'What are you doing?' she whispered in a frantic under- tone.

One dark eyebrow lifted wryly. 'It looks like I'm bail- ing you out of a mess,' he said. 'It seems you have spun Molly's grandparents quite a story.'

Carrie cringed. 'It wasn't intentional,' she whispered hurriedly. 'Carmel wanted to know who you were when she saw you in that taxi. And I didn't like to say you were just some stranger I'd met on a plane so I said you were a boyfriend. It was a moment of madness…' Her voice was husky and urgent, her eyes wide and pleading with him for understanding. 'I was desperate to convince her that my life was settled—but I was wrong to lie, I know that now. She took it far too seriously and before I knew what was happening you went from fake boyfriend to fake fiancé in the space of five minutes.'

Max grinned. 'Pretty giant step for a bachelor career girl.'

'You're not kidding.' Carrie nodded, then glanced into the dining room to check if Carmel and Bob were waiting for them. Luckily they seemed deep in conversation with one of the waiters. 'I'd planned to own up to the truth today. So really there's no point you hanging around.' She looked back at him. 'Once I've explained everything and calmed Carmel, hopefully she will come around to my way of thinking.'

'Or she might not.' Max took in the way Carrie's skin blanched white at those words, the way her arms instinctively tightened on the little girl in her arms.

'No, she might not,' Carrie admitted shakily.

Max was silent for a moment. 'So I could help you out here—go along with this charade of yours for a few days—or weeks—until Molly's grandparents have gone back to Australia.' His voice was thoughtful; his eyes held hers with dark, serious intent. 'And in return you could help me out of a similar problem.'

'In what way? I don't understand.'

Before Max could answer Carmel suddenly appeared at the doorway. 'What are you two talking about out here? We've got a table for five by the window.'

'Won't be a moment, Carmel,' Carrie said.

'So what do you say?' Max asked in a hushed undertone beside her. 'Have we got an agreement?'

Carrie hesitated, trying to think sensibly, but all she could see were Carmel's sharp eyes watching them across the hallway and all she could think of was that for now this would solve her immediate problems.

'Yes,' she said impulsively and firmly. 'Yes, we've got an agreement.'

CHAPTER FOUR

MOLLY seemed to have settled quite happily in the chair between Max and Carrie.

'Carrie was telling us you live on a vineyard, Max?' Carmel was asking as she poured him some tea.

'Yes, the Santos vinery.' Max reached to help Molly choose a cake from the stand. 'It's a family business.'

'How lovely—and is that where you and Carrie will live when you get married?'

Carrie almost choked on her tea at that question, but Max seemed to take the subject in his stride.

'Oh, I imagine so.' Max glanced across at Carrie and saw the expression in her eyes. He smiled. 'What do you say, darling? You like it at the vineyard, don't you?'

'It's beautiful up there,' Carrie said hastily. 'Lot's of space,' she added, trying to sound as relaxed as Max. But she couldn't help feeling she was failing miserably. She hated this. Max was her business client. Lying to Carmel and Bob was wrong. It was all incredibly wrong. Of course she could give Molly a good life, whether there was a man on the scene or not. And at the back of her mind she kept wondering what it was that Max wanted her to do for him in return.

'You know, Carrie, I've suddenly noticed that you aren't wearing an engagement ring,' Carmel said, leaning forward.

'Have you?' Carrie stared at her left hand, taken aback by the observation, and her brain seemed to freeze in panic as she searched for some excuse. 'Well, that's, eh, that's—'

'That's because up until now we've kept the engagement a secret,' Max interrupted her smoothly. 'We've been waiting for things to settle down a little before announcing our intentions.'

Carmel frowned. 'Settle down in what way?'

'It's been a traumatic time for Carrie and Molly, these last few months, Carmel,' Max said gently. 'Carrie hasn't exactly felt like celebrating.'

'I can understand that...' Carmel glanced across at Carrie, her expression sympathetic.

'But we are ready to announce our engagement now, aren't we, darling?' Max smiled across at her.

'Yes...I think we should.' Carrie hoped her voice didn't sound as panicky as she felt. She had never felt more uncomfortable in her life.

'So when are you thinking of setting a date for the big day?' Carmel asked insistently, fixing Max with a sharp, intent expression.

'We are just taking our time over everything,' Carrie interrupted hastily, wanting this line of enquiry to stop. 'We have to think about Molly first now.'

Carmel seemed to consider this for a moment. 'Yes, but you shouldn't put off your wedding date. The sooner things are settled for you and Max, the better it will be for Molly. I like the sound of this vineyard, don't you, Bob?'

She glanced over at her husband, who nodded. He looked tired, Carrie thought, feeling sudden sympathy for the man. He was obviously jet-lagged after the flight from Australia.

'Sarah...that's Molly's mother,' he explained to Max, 'was our only child. We still miss her greatly. We do want to do our best for Molly.' He seemed to draw himself up in his chair with difficulty. 'But bringing up a small child is a demanding job. I'm not very well, and when my wife told me we should have Molly, I have to be honest, I worried about how we'd cope—how Carmel would cope. Things have not been easy for her, looking after me—'

'Bob!' Carmel cut across his speech crossly. 'Of course we'd cope. We'd just *have* to cope; it's our duty to Sarah. We've been through this a hundred times. We are Molly's closest blood relatives...' Carmel shot a look over at Carrie. 'No offence, Carrie, but Tony was only your half-brother.'

The words struck fear into Carrie; she had half feared that Carmel might use this fact to get Molly. 'Yes, but we were close, Carmel,' she said hastily.

'But we have the closer blood tie. And we would be capable of looking after her—'

'Yes, of course we'd cope.' Bob cut his wife off in mid-speech. 'But if we are both to be honest taking our granddaughter to live with us isn't our first choice. We know we'd find it hard to adjust. For one thing, she hardly knows us. Plus, a youngster takes lots of energy and time.' He fixed Carrie with a stern, long look. 'Obviously she adores you. I could see that the way she clung to you out there in the foyer. But if we are going to hand her over we need to know she will not come second after a multitude of boyfriends and a career that takes you away all the time. Meeting Max today has at least taken away some of that fear.'

Carrie could feel herself growing hotter and more disconcerted by the second. She really empathised with what this man was saying. 'I promise you I will always put Molly first,' she said huskily, her blue eyes wide and sincere as they held with his. At least that was the truth, no matter about Max or living on vineyards, or her job—or anything. Molly would come first.

Max glanced across Molly's head and saw the expression in Carrie's eyes, saw the way she held herself ramrod-straight in the chair. He could see that she hated this deception. He could see that she was desperately sorry for Molly's grandparents and wanted to reassure them, to make everything all right for them as well as Molly.

Bob nodded and then looked over at Max. 'That's all right, then. In the meantime we'll hang around a little, get to know Molly, take her out and we'll see how things go. Perhaps we could come up to your vineyard one day.'

Carrie felt her heart lurch crazily.

'By all means,' Max agreed easily.

The waiter arrived at the table to clear away some of the plates of sandwiches and brought Molly's ice cream.

For a moment all the adults watched as she tucked into it happily.

'Is that nice, darling?' Carrie asked her, and she nodded and then grinned. Perhaps it was something about the child's innocent pleasure, or maybe it was the aftermath of the conversation with her grandparents, Carrie didn't know, but suddenly she could feel tears welling up inside her.

She met Max's eyes and smiled, determined to keep herself together, and then was extremely relieved when Max started up a conversation about the vineyard, chatting easily to Bob, telling him that they would be taking in the grapes soon, and then talking about the business generally. The normality of the conversation was a balm to Carrie's senses. And Bob and Carmel were extremely interested.

Max was quite funny as well. He told them about amusing incidents and talked about other members of his family and their roles in the upkeep of the estate. Carrie watched as the lines of tension softened on Molly's grand-mother's face. And Bob seemed to get a new lease of energy as he helped himself for the first time to some of the cake on the china plates in front of him. Even Molly chuckled as Max included her in the conversation, by occasionally bringing a story down to a silly level that she could understand, making her eyes shine with merriment.

By the time the waiters had come to clear all the empty dishes away the atmosphere at the table was light-hearted. Molly had finished her ice cream and had pink raspberry all over her hands and her mouth. Carrie reached to tidy her up with one of the napkins as much as she could and then picked her up off the chair to take her to the cloak-room. 'Excuse us,' she said with a smile. 'I'm just going to wash Molly's hands before we get ice cream on her dress.'

Carmel watched as the two crossed the busy dining room. Then looked over at Max. 'I'm so pleased Carrie has met you,' she said impulsively. 'From what Tony told me, that first husband of hers was a complete rat. Tony used to worry about her a lot at that time, although he did say she had been happier since coming to live in Spain and that she was dating again. He never said she was seeing someone as settled and family-orientated as you, though...' Carmel frowned. 'In fact the last time we spoke on the phone and he mentioned Carrie I got the impression her latest boyfriend was someone she worked with at the office.'

'Carmel!' Her husband frowned and shook his head. 'You probably only got half a story,' he admonished. 'All of your conversations with Tony were about Molly.'

'Yes...yes, of course.' Carmel started to look a bit red in the face. 'I just meant to say that it's wonderful that you two have met, and Carrie is a lovely girl—she deserves some happiness after that horrible husband.'

Max digested this information and then tried to soothe Carmel as she flustered on, telling him she had probably misunderstood Tony. 'You didn't get it completely wrong,' he said as Carmel paused to catch her breath. 'Carrie and I did meet through work. She's doing an advertising campaign for the vineyard.'

'Oh, I see.' Carmel looked immediately relieved. Then smiled at him. 'She's very attractive, isn't she?'

'Yes, very,' Max agreed with a grin. He looked up and noticed Carrie returning. He watched the way she moved across the room towards them. He liked the graceful way she walked, the confidence and the gentleness in her manner. He also noticed the way the other men in the room glanced at her with appreciation as she passed, something she seemed totally oblivious of. And he wondered suddenly about the man she had been dating in the office.

'We were just talking about how you and Max met,' Carmel said as Carrie reached the table.

'Really?' Carrie smiled, but she could feel the muscles aching on her face as she tried to keep the expression in place. She glanced over at Max, willing him to enlighten her as to what story he had been spinning while she'd been away.

'I was just saying that it was work-related—that you were organising a brilliant advertising campaign for the vineyard,' he said smoothly.

'Oh…yes.' Carrie nodded.

Carmel smiled. 'I met Bob at work as well. We'll have been married forty years next December.'

'Congratulations,' Max said sincerely.

Carmel nodded. 'It was love at first sight. As soon as

we met we just knew we were meant for each other. Was it the same for you two?'

Carrie tried to avoid looking over at Max as embarrassment flooded through her. She felt as if all credibility for their business relationship was disappearing fast, and she wished the ground would open up and swallow her. 'Well, you know, Carmel, it wasn't really like that,' she murmured. 'It was business and...' She floundered, not knowing what else to say.

'And it was destiny.' Max rescued her with a smooth ease. 'As soon as our eyes met we both knew there was something very special between us.'

Carrie glanced over at him, marvelling at the way he was able to sound so charmingly sincere. As her eyes met his dark intense gaze she felt her blood starting to race through her veins. And for a moment, a brief, silly moment, she wondered what it would be like if that were true. If this whole charade were for real. The warmth of that thought sent her senses spinning. Hurriedly she looked away from him again.

This was all an act, and Max was convincing because he was a charmer. A man who knew exactly how to make a woman feel special just with a mere smile—just like her ex-husband. She couldn't afford the luxury of forgetting that; there were too many things at stake here, both personally and professionally.

Carrie cleared her throat. She had to get out of here, away from these lies. As Molly tried to make her way back to her chair beside Max, Carrie caught hold of her hand and stopped her. 'We really have to be going now,' she said firmly, looking from Carmel to Bob. 'I have to get Molly back home for her siesta. And I'm sure you could do with some rest after your long flight, Bob.'

Bob nodded and everyone got to their feet.

'Nice meeting you, Max. We'll look forward to our next get-together,' Carmel said happily. 'And we'll ring you later, Carrie, about coming over to see Molly.'

Carrie nodded. 'Yes, whenever you like,' she agreed.

The relief of stepping outside the hotel was immeasurable, even though the heat of the afternoon was stifling.

Carrie felt emotionally drained; all she wanted was her apartment and a cold drink. As the doorman stepped forward to offer to get them a cab Max put a detaining hand on her arm. 'Come on, my car is around the corner,' he said briskly. And before she could say anything he was leading her towards the entrance to an underground car park. Molly was hopping from foot to foot and pulling against Carrie's hand and she stopped to pick her up, to keep her safe from any cars that might be pulling out.

'Here, give her to me,' Max said. 'She's too heavy for you to carry down these steps to the car.'

Molly went across to him without a murmur and grinned at Carrie from over his shoulder as if this was all great fun.

Max's car was a black BMW. He unlocked it with a flick of a button and then secured Molly into the back seat with the seat belt. As Carrie relaxed into the passenger seat beside him he turned on the air-conditioning and opened the fans so that they were directed onto her. 'That better?' he asked.

She nodded.

His eyes raked over the pallor of her countenance with concern. 'Was the heat getting to you?'

'The heat of the situation was worse. I felt so awful lying to them, Max.'

'If it's any consolation, they looked a lot happier when we left,' he said gently.

'Yes, but somehow that just made me feel even more

guilty.' Carrie leaned her head back against the car seat and closed her eyes for a second. 'Wasn't it just appalling?' she said in a hushed undertone. 'I should have told the truth.'

'I think what you did was kinder in the long run,' Max said seriously. 'You've relieved them of a heavy weight of responsibility. They obviously love their grandchild, but Bob didn't look well. And even Carmel was looking more and more relieved as she realised you had things in hand here.'

'I still don't feel good about it.' Carrie opened her eyes and looked over at him. 'But I have to say you deserve an Oscar for your part. Thank you.'

'We made an agreement, Carrie,' he said nonchalantly. 'You just return the favour for me and we'll call it even.'

The cool response disconcerted her slightly. He turned the key in the ignition and the powerful engine hummed into life.

'So what exactly is this favour?' she asked curiously.

He turned the car out of the parking space and up into the bright sunlight of the day before answering. 'What I need is a similar acting job with my family.' He flicked a wry glance over at her. 'We'll interlock. You pretend to be my fiancée, I pretend to be yours; a nice businesslike arrangement that will make everyone happy.'

He sounded like her boss José, when he was closing a deal. Only this wasn't business, this was playing with people's emotions, and Carrie felt more than a twinge of misgiving. 'I don't understand. Why do you need a fiancée?'

'My father has found out Manuel is leaving. And the timing couldn't be worse. He's started talking about going back into the office, says he will go back as soon as they discharge him from the hospital on Monday.' Max stopped the car at some traffic lights and drummed his fingertips on the steering wheel. 'I've told him not to worry, that I will take over, but he's stubbornly refusing to accept the offer. He says that I haven't got the passion for the land. That if I had I would have settled down with a nice girl and raised a family.' He glanced across at Carrie with a look of grim concern in his eyes. 'The specialist has told my mother that if he goes back to the pressures of work his health will diminish rapidly. She's worried sick…we all are.'

The traffic lights changed. 'Which way to your apartment?' Max asked, ignoring the blare of horns behind them as he paused.

'You need to turn left at the next junction.' She watched as he manoeuvred through the busy lanes of cars. 'So you think if you introduce me as your fiancée that your father will feel better about handing things over to you?'

'It will prove to him that I'm serious about taking over. Which I am, incidentally.' Max glanced over at her. 'But having you on side will help convince him of that; it will buy some time, stop him fretting.'

'Yes, but it's just a pretence, Max.' She shook her head. 'How will your father feel when you tell him a little while later that our fake engagement is off?'

'I suppose he'll feel the same as Carmel and Bob will,' Max said. 'But he'll just have to get over it. These things happen. Relationships fail. We just have to deal with it and move on.'

Carrie glanced over at him, noting the hard edge, the quiet inevitability to those words. Max Santos was obviously a realist; he'd weighed up the pros and cons in a coolly businesslike way and had decided that the end justified the means. She wondered if it was his high-flying job that had given him that forceful edge, or something else—something more personal from his past.

'Which is why I suggest we just keep up the pretence for as long as we can...' Max continued crisply. 'That way we are buying time and, I know it's a cliché, but time is a healer. In that space my father can rest, and Carmel and Bob can come to terms with Tony's death and this change of circumstances.'

Carrie didn't say anything for a moment. What he had said made a kind of sense. Seeing how Carmel and Bob had relaxed around Max today had made everything seem normal and under control, and for a while the lifting of tension had been a blissful relief.

'It almost sounds practical when you put it like that,' she murmured.

'I think it is practical,' Max said firmly. 'We are both single, and neither of us wants a heavy commitment. This arrangement could work perfectly. Unless, of course, you have a boyfriend somewhere in the background who is going to kick up a fuss.'

'No, there is no boyfriend,' Carrie said quietly.

'So no skeletons are going to fall out of closets, then?' he persisted. 'It's just that Carmel mentioned over lunch that Tony had told her you were dating someone in the office.'

He glanced over and noticed how her skin suddenly flushed with colour. She pointed up ahead to a road that led off the main thoroughfare. 'I live down there,' she told him stiffly.

Max turned into her road and followed her directions to pull the car up outside a tall, narrow townhouse with an ornate terrazzo entrance.

He turned off the engine and then turned to look at her. 'So are you seeing someone at work?'

Her blue eyes darkened angrily. 'My private life is my business,' she muttered. 'Nobody has the right to pry. Not Carmel. Not you—'

'Carrie, if we are going to go through with this arrangement we both need to know where we stand.' He cut across her with firm determination. 'Unless, of course, you've changed your mind and you want to ring Carmel and Bob, tell them the truth.'

The prospect filled Carrie with a cold, clammy, sick feeling. She glanced over into the back seat of the car. Molly was fast asleep, her head resting against Mojo's. She remembered how scared the little girl had been in the hotel foyer. How she had clung to her trembling and sobbing. Carrie was the only familiar figure in her life at the moment. Molly needed her. 'No, I don't want to change my mind.' She glanced back at Max. 'Yes, I was seeing someone at work—my boss José. But he couldn't accept the fact that Molly has to come first in my life now, and things have changed.'

'Changed as in the affair has ended?'

Max's dark eyes seemed to be raking into her very soul. She nodded.

Max watched her, sensed how much she hated letting him inside her life even this much. It was as if she was scared of opening up to him, as if she had big orange traffic cones around her saying, You can only come so far with me. I'm my own person.

Then she lifted her chin and fixed him with that confident 'I'm in charge' look that he recognised from their business lunch. 'So what about you?' she asked crisply. 'Why are you asking *me* to pose as your fiancée? There must be a million women you could ask. You could even propose to someone for real, settle down.'

'I decided to do that once before.' His voice softened

suddenly. 'I was engaged. Everything was in place for our wedding, but...' He shrugged. 'It just didn't work out.'

There was a hint of wistfulness in his tone for a moment, a serious look in his dark eyes that made her wonder what had happened between him and his ex-fiancée. And she remembered his stark words earlier. *'Relationships fail. We just have to deal with it and move on.'*

Did Max have regrets about the past?

Before she could ask him anything he switched briskly back to a practical tone. 'So, you see, I think it's best that I stick to a more businesslike arrangement this time.'

The blunt statement made Carrie think he probably did have regrets. That, like her, he had decided it was better to be single.

'I suppose this kind of agreement has its pluses,' she said hesitantly. 'Neither of us will get hurt.'

'Exactly. It's the perfect deal,' Max agreed. 'I'm helping you out; you're helping me. It's a sensible arrangement. With no strings.'

Something about the way he emphasised the last point, in a brisk, pragmatic tone, grated on her. 'Yes, okay, Max, I get the point,' she said coolly. 'And you have no need to worry on that score, I can assure you. I'm not going to get carried away by the pretence. I have absolutely no wish to get married again.'

'So, as I said before, it's the perfect arrangement,' Max said lightly. His gaze moved from the fire in her blue eyes to the gentle curve of her lips. 'But of course we will have to be convincing in our parts.'

She looked at him warily. 'What do you mean?'

'I mean that people will expect us to act like lovers. Not as business partners.'

Hastily she looked away from him, the softly spoken words sending all kinds of alarm bells ringing inside her.

'As long as we are civil with each other. And say the right things when needed—like today—I think that will be enough…'

Max reached out suddenly and put a hand under her chin, tipping her face up so that she was forced to look at him. The gentle contact sent her emotions into complete chaos. 'I think people will expect a little more than that,' he said huskily.

'A little more in what way?' she murmured. She could feel her heart drumming against her chest so powerfully that it made her feel dizzy.

His eyes moved to the softness of her lips again and suddenly Carrie felt the emotional temperature between them spiral out of control.

He moved closer and she knew he was going to kiss her. Her instincts were telling her to move back and yet she couldn't. She was held by a force that was much more powerful than anything her mind was telling her; this was almost primal, it was so overwhelming.

As he moved closer the scent of his cologne crept into her senses, warm and clean and somehow extremely provocative. His fingertips traced the side of her face, sending shivery little messages of desire shooting through to her very nerve-endings. Then his lips moved to capture hers.

The touch was electric. At first the kiss was gentle, provocatively teasing. She responded uncertainly, trying with all her strength to fight the dark forces that were urging her to move closer, that were whispering encouraging little words deep inside about how wonderful this felt. Then his lips became more demanding; they plundered hers with a hunger that sent the last semblance of rationality flying from her mind. She wanted this. Wanted it to go on and on. And she responded heatedly, her body rejoicing as she felt his arms closing around her, pulling her even closer. The kiss was mind-blowing and devastating. Exciting beyond belief.

A sound from the back seat of the car made them pull apart hurriedly. Carrie glanced around. Molly was still asleep; she had just rearranged herself so that her head was resting on the window of the door.

'She's okay.' Max was the first to speak.

'Yes...' Carrie glanced back at him and the memory of that kiss seemed to dance in the air between them like some kind of taunt. She felt mortified. What the hell had just happened?

He smiled at her gently. 'Well, looks like we won't have too much difficulty playing the part of lovers after all,' he said teasingly.

Carrie swallowed hard. 'I'd better go, Max. Molly needs her bed.' As she got out of the car Max followed her.

'I'll carry her in for you,' he offered as she looked across at him questioningly. 'That way maybe you can get her down without waking her.'

She hesitated for a second and then nodded. At least if Molly had a sleep now it would give her time to gather herself together and think about the direction that her life was suddenly veering off in.

Carrie watched as he opened the back door of the car and then reached gently across to unfasten the sleeping child from the safety belt. Molly stirred but she didn't wake up.

Opening her handbag, Carrie found her front-door keys and led the way through the door and then up the mosaic-tiled stairway towards her apartment on the first floor.

She unlocked it and then moved down her hall and into the small bedroom that was Molly's.

'Thank you,' she said as she watched Max put her down into the bed.

'That's all right,' Max said. 'She's a lovely little girl— reminds me of my sister's child, Belle.'

'I didn't know you had a sister.' Carrie turned to adjust the blinds so that the room was in semi-darkness.

'Yes, Victoria—you met her children the other day at my house. Belle and Emilio.'

'I thought they were your estate manager's children? Oh, I see,' Carrie said suddenly as comprehension dawned. 'Manuel is your brother-in-law as well as Estate Manager?'

'Former Estate Manager, as it turns out,' Max said wryly. 'But, yes, Manuel is my brother-in-law. We've a lot to find out about each other now that we are getting engaged, don't you think?' he added softly. 'A lot of catching up.'

Carrie knew he was speaking in a low tone so as not to wake Molly, but the husky undertone sent flutters of awareness shooting through her. And the half-light of the room seemed suddenly disturbingly personal. She found herself thinking about that kiss in the car. The level of passion that had sprung between them from nowhere had been shockingly intense; her body was still reeling from it.

Irritated by the reaction, she reminded herself sharply that a few minutes before he had kissed her he had been emphasising the fact that this was just a business deal. So any passion that had flared between them was in her imagination. It was just a kiss, no big deal.

'How about dinner tomorrow night?' he asked.

Carrie remembered he had asked her the same question when she had bumped into him at the reception desk at the hotel this morning. And she had refused him. Firstly because she hadn't wanted Molly's grandparents to think she worked and was away from Molly in the evenings. And secondly because she wanted to keep her dealings with Max strictly within the safety confines of business. But both those reasons no longer held up.

'Well, I suppose we do still need to talk about work anyway,' she said cautiously, trying to sound practical. 'You were saying something this morning about some queries you had about the advertising contract?'

'Yes, I was...' Max sounded dryly amused, as if her returning to the subject of work half irritated him. 'So, shall I pick you up tomorrow night? Say about seven-thirty?'

'I'll have to check with Carmel and Bob to see if they have any plans for Molly...'

'Why don't you ask them to babysit?' Max suggested. 'They might like to do that, and we could go to a restaurant nearby—that way we can return here quickly if there is any problem.'

'Okay, I'll ask them,' she found herself agreeing. Dinner with Max did sound appealing. There was a part of her that wanted to know him better. A part that was fascinated by him. She wondered if it was the same kind of fascination that children sometimes felt with fire. 'And we can discuss business,' she added again firmly. 'I'll bring a copy of the contract and we can go through it.'

'I'm sure Carmel and Bob would be very interested to see you going out with your fiancé for the evening with your briefcase,' Max said firmly. 'For once, Carrie, leave work at home.' The sentence was more like a command than a request. 'We're going out tomorrow on a date. Any talk about work can be dealt with in the first twenty minutes.'

'But I thought you were anxious to get the contract

rolling...' Carrie found that she was talking to herself. Max had turned and left the room.

Hurriedly she followed him towards the front door.

'Max, I...'

'I'll pick you up tomorrow at seven-thirty,' he said. 'See you then.' He reached and touched her face. It was just a gentle caress, as if he was satisfied that he had got his own way, yet it set her skin on fire.

As the door closed behind him Carrie leaned back against it.

Since her divorce she had prided herself on being in control of her life. Having everything orderly and controllable, be it work or relationships... Now suddenly her life seemed to be pulling her along in the weirdest of directions and she felt as if she were losing the reins of power over her own destiny. It was scary, but even more frightening was the memory of that kiss a few minutes ago and the effect it had had.

CHAPTER FIVE

WHAT did a woman wear for a fake date with a fake fiancé? Carrie wondered as she riffled through her wardrobe for what seemed like the millionth time.

She took out a long white dress and held it up against herself. It had a plunging neckline. Too revealing. She discarded it and reached for a floral dress—somehow that seemed too frothy and feminine.

Decisively she took out the black dress again. That would have to do. It was smart, yet attractive, could pass for business or pleasure. Yes, the black dress was the safest option.

Her mind made up, she sat down at the dressing table and dried her hair. From the lounge she could hear the TV. Carmel and Bob had arrived early to look after Molly.

They were really very kind people, Carrie thought. Molly was still a bit wary around them, but she seemed happy in the familiar surroundings of the flat. She had eaten her tea happily with them earlier, and then Carmel had helped get her ready for bed. Although Molly was now fast asleep Carrie was glad that Max had suggested a restaurant nearby, just in case Carmel and Bob had any problems.

Carrie reached for her make-up and applied a very light cyclamen-pink lipstick. Then slipped into the black dress. The effect was pleasing; the dress emphasised her slender figure and the light golden colour of her hair. Picking up her black beaded handbag, she made her way out into the living room.

'You look lovely, Carrie,' Carmel said immediately.

'Thank you.' Carrie smiled at her and then looked over at Bob, who was fast asleep in the chair.

'That long flight has taken a lot out of him,' Carmel said as she followed Carrie's gaze. 'And his health isn't one hundred per cent.'

'If he wants to go to bed the spare room is made up.' Carrie sat down on the settee. 'That goes for you too, Carmel. You both need to take things easy,' she said. 'Tony's death has taken its toll on us all.'

'You're right, and worrying about Molly hasn't helped.' Carmel turned down the volume of the TV. 'I think we will have an early night. I'm so relieved that you have met such a nice man, Carrie. We both thought Max was wonderful. I can't tell you the peace of mind it has brought us, just knowing that Molly is settled and happy with you both. Because I suppose, if I'm being honest, Bob was right yesterday when he said we were worried about how we would have coped with her—not that we wouldn't have managed, of course,' she finished, with a return of her old spirited determination.

'Of course,' Carrie said gently. 'And I do understand that you only want the best for your granddaughter.'

The doorbell rang. 'That will be Max.' Carrie glanced at her watch and noticed he was exactly on time. 'Now, you've got my mobile number—if you need anything don't hesitate to ring me.'

'I won't. You just have a lovely romantic time with that handsome man of yours.'

Carrie went to answer the door. A lovely romantic time was not what she needed or wanted, she reminded herself stiffly. That kiss yesterday had meant nothing, and the fact that she kept remembering it at the oddest moments was really irritating her. First thing on her agenda this evening was to make sure that this arrangement with Max wasn't going to mess things up business-wise between them. José would be expecting her to have things with the Santos vineyard pretty much wrapped up next week.

And her job was important; she was going to be relying on it now more than ever to support Molly.

Her mind rationalised and her confidence high, she opened the door.

Max was wearing a dark blue suit with a pale blue shirt. As always he had that continental flair, looking effortlessly stylish. But it was the way he looked at her that made her heart stand still, that made her sensible thoughts melt away. His dark eyes held hers in a way that was all male—and extremely compelling. It made her remember the way he had kissed her, the way she had craved to be closer to him. It set a thunderous, clamorous need racing inside her.

'Hello, Max.' With determination she made her voice extremely cool.

He smiled at her. 'You look lovely, Carrie.'

Even the way he said her name made tingles of awareness shoot through her. Furious with herself after all her wise words of counsel, she looked away. 'Thank you; step inside for a moment.' Politely she stood back to allow him in. 'I just want to have a quick check on Molly before we go.'

'How is she today?' he asked.

'Fine. Carmel and Bob came round early and they all got on very well.' As she was speaking she was moving away from him towards Molly's bedroom door.

She crept quietly in. Molly was still fast asleep, her toy dog tightly tucked under one arm, her lips slightly curved in a small smile.

Looking down at her, Carrie tried to assure herself that

her pretence with Max was worthwhile. Everything was going to work out.

But when she returned to the hallway and Max put a light hand against her back to guide her out of the door the same feelings of panic reared up inside her again. The feeling that she wasn't in control here. He was.

The night air was warm and slightly humid, and Max's car was parked just outside the front door. He opened the passenger door for her before going around to the driver's side.

For a moment there was silence as he started the engine and pulled out into the road.

'Have they released your father from hospital yet?' Carrie asked.

'No, but they will tomorrow afternoon hopefully.'

'That's good. Your mother must be relieved.'

'Yes, she is.'

'And have you mentioned anything about me?'

'No.'

She glanced across at him, wondering if he had changed his mind about the agreement. His face was in darkness, only lit from time to time by the passing headlights of cars. It was hard to gauge what he was thinking. 'Are you going to mention me?' she asked tentatively. 'Or have you changed your mind?' It was strange—one part of her was vehemently against lies of any kind, and yet thinking he might be pulling out of the agreement gave her an equally cold feeling in the pit of her stomach.

Max didn't answer her straight away; instead he pulled the car around the corner and into a car-parking space. Only when he had switched off the engine and the lights did he turn to look at her. 'I think we should be seen out together a lot more before I mention you,' he said decisively. 'That's why I have chosen this restaurant for dinner tonight. Apart from it being close to your apartment it is frequented by people I know; family members and friends alike tend to congregate here. It will make our affair more realistic if other people report it back to my parents. That way they might ask me about you...' he shrugged '...and then, when I "own up," they will feel delighted. It will make everything much more believable.'

'I see.' Carrie was quiet for a moment. 'You are very good at this deception caper,' she said thoughtfully.

'It's important we get it right,' Max said, reaching for the door handle. 'And if we have a few dates at the right places it will help to set the scene. My father is a shrewd man; he knows me too well to be taken in lightly.'

Carrie followed him out of the car. She wondered if by knowing him well Max meant his father knew he was a man who only liked to play the field. The thought sat uneasily inside her. She wanted to cast it aside and think of him as the charmingly tender man who had comforted Molly at the hotel yesterday and had been so playful and fun with his sister's children at lunch the other day.

And if she were being honest there was also a part of her that wanted to believe that the way he had kissed her yesterday might have meant something. But she knew that was naive in the extreme. Max had gone out of his way to emphasise the point that this was only a business arrangement. And the kiss had only been intended as a test to make sure that they could convincingly play the part of lovers. She couldn't afford to forget that and get fact and fantasy mixed in her mind. This was business.

Although it was almost eight the streets of Barcelona were crowded with shoppers. The lights that spilled from the windows were welcoming and golden, and the buzz of conversation reassuringly normal. This was the way it always was in the city. People had a siesta in the heat of the day and then worked late, shopped late, and seemed to live life at a busy, more energetic pace when the sun went down. Carrie loved the buzz of this city, loved the ornate architecture, the galleries and shops and parks. Life here seemed so civilised somehow.

It was also a city of excellent cuisine, and the restaurant that Max led her towards had one of the best reputations in town.

'How did you get a reservation here at such short notice?' she asked as he pushed the door open and stood back for her to precede him.

'I come quite often. Plus I know the owner.'

'Is he a family member?' Carrie asked with a smile.

'Ambrosio is my cousin.' He grinned. 'His father works up at the vineyard.'

The restaurant had low lighting and candles flickered in the individual private booths. The ambience was one of intimate relaxation, yet it was stylishly trendy, making it the kind of place that people liked to be seen.

The receptionist, an attractive brunette in her early thirties, greeted Max warmly. She came around the desk and stood on the tiptoes of red stiletto heels to kiss him on both cheeks, enquiring after his father's health and listening to his reply with a look of deep attentiveness in her dark eyes. They talked for a moment about his father, and then Max quickly switched to speaking English as he turned to introduce Carrie. 'Carrie, this is my cousin's wife, Estelle.'

Carrie was conscious of the way the other woman quickly weighed her up, with a look that was boldly, almost brutally assessing. But her voice when she spoke was perfectly polite. 'I'm pleased to meet you, Carrie. I have a good memory for faces and I'm sure we have seen you in here before.'

'Yes, a few times,' Carrie murmured. 'Your food is always excellent.'

'Thank you; my husband Ambrosio is the chef as well as the owner of the establishment. He is very talented. Let me take you to your table.' As they walked down the wide aisle towards the side of the restaurant Carrie noticed how the other woman linked her arm through Max's. She had a very beautiful figure and she seemed to sway her hips as she walked, the red dress she wore emphasising her perfect curves. Before they reached their table she reached up and said something close to Max's ear.

Carrie tried to ignore it, tried to pretend she wasn't even curious about what she might have said. The woman was Max's cousin's wife, so it couldn't have been anything too personal, surely? Probably just a bit of family repartee. Even so, Carrie couldn't help feeling pleased when Max pulled away from her and instead turned to wait, so that he could allow Carrie to settle into the small private booth before taking his seat opposite.

Estelle handed them both a menu and then lingered beside them for a moment. Carrie had the impression that she was waiting for Max to ask her to join them; the atmosphere seemed a bit odd.

'Thank you, Estelle.' Max's voice was pleasant, but dismissive.

She smiled a bright, almost brittle smile and left them.

'What was that all about?' Carrie asked curiously.

'Just Estelle being nosy. She's a terrible gossip and will want all the details about you so she can pass them on to the rest of the family.'

'Oh, I see.' Carrie smiled, a flickering light of amusement in her blue eyes. 'Which I suppose is why you brought me here. So, tell me, do you think I've passed the first test?'

'Absolutely.' Something about the serious way he answered her light-hearted remark made her stomach dip as if she were on a fairground ride. For a moment his eyes held with hers.

Then Max picked up the wine menu. 'So what would you like to drink?' he asked.

'Santos wine, of course,' Carrie said lightly.

'Hey, we are leaving work behind tonight,' he admonished with a grin. 'So I suggest we try some of the opposition's offerings.'

'Then I'll leave the wine selection to you,' she said.

As Max perused the wine list Carrie tried to concentrate on the menu, but she kept glancing over at him, distracted by his presence. The candlelight threw flickering shadows over his ruggedly handsome face. She wondered what it would be like to really date Max, for him to be genuinely interested in her. Her eyes moved towards his lips, remembering how compelling and demanding they had felt against hers. No one had ever stirred such fervid hunger inside her with just one kiss before.

He glanced up and caught her watching him. 'Have you made your decision already?' he asked.

Rather than say she had been too busy thinking about him, she nodded.

He signalled the waiter to take their order and hurriedly she selected the first things that caught her eye on the printed lists.

Carrie noticed how easily Max switched from speaking Spanish to English as they were left alone again.

'Your English is perfect,' she remarked. 'I've noticed a few times how you never seem to struggle searching for a word, which I sometimes do when speaking Spanish.'

'I think your Spanish is excellent,' Max said. 'And your accent is extremely sensual.'

Usually Carrie would have had no problem laughing a remark like that off, but something about the way Max spoke, the way he looked her directly in the eye, made it hard to keep herself from blushing. 'I get by at work and that's the main thing,' she managed to say matter-of-factly, then swiftly turned the conversation back to him. 'Where did you learn to speak English?'

'My mother is English. She met my father when she came over for a holiday to visit friends. Apparently the day they met was the day she should have been flying home, but her flight was cancelled so her friends took her to a party that evening instead. She always says that it was destiny. They were meant to meet. And my father says that as soon as he saw her he knew instantly that she was the woman he wanted to marry.'

Carrie smiled, charmed by the story. 'It was love at first sight. A little like Carmel and Bob. I've often wondered about that. I can understand attraction at first sight, yes. But how do you know someone is right for you...I mean *really* right for you just by looking at them—when you don't even know them?' She shrugged, 'I can't imagine ever feeling that sure of anything.'

'If you were to ask my mother about that she would say you just know. You feel it inside.' He put a hand on the middle of his chest. 'She says that you feel it right about here. That it strikes hard and it just gets you.' He smiled teasingly. 'And apparently before you know it you are hooked and reeled in.'

His smile seemed to do very strange things to Carrie's heart. 'Your mum is a bit of a romantic, isn't she?' she murmured lightly.

'Just a bit.' He grinned. 'Even now after all these years she will tell that story with passion. And they have been through some difficult times but always stood solidly together, so maybe she is right and sometimes you should just trust your instincts.'

'Maybe.' Carrie shrugged. 'I used to be a bit of a romantic myself…' She trailed off, wishing she hadn't said that.

'But not now?'

Carrie thought about that question for a moment. Once upon a time she would have said yes, categorically, she was a romantic. But that was before she had married Martin, before she had discovered what everyone else around her had known long before her. Yes, she had witnessed how women had gravitated towards him. And, yes, she had seen how he had flirted with them, but naively she hadn't realised how far he had taken those dalliances. 'I think I'm more of a realist these days,' she said.

She was glad that the waiter arrived at that moment and poured the wine for Max to taste.

'So what is the verdict on the wine?' she asked him once they were left alone again, glad to get the subject back to something neutral. 'How does it compare with the Santos estate?'

'It's high quality but not as outstanding.' He gave her a boyish smile. 'Of course.'

She smiled back and then lifted her glass, pretending to inhale the scent emanating from within. 'I see what you mean,' she said with mock seriousness. 'Even the bouquet isn't as good.' She took a small sip. 'But it is very palatable; I like the subtle hint of blackberry. It's rather a cheeky little number, isn't it?'

Max laughed. 'We'll make a wine expert out of you yet,' he said. 'My parents will be pleased.'

She smiled back. 'Tell me about the rest of your family. How many brothers and sisters do you have?'

'Just the one sister, Victoria,' said Max. 'I did have an

older brother, Ramon. He should have been the one taking over the vineyard, but he died ten years ago. So it falls to me.' There was a calm tone to his voice that nevertheless failed to disguise an element of sadness.

'I'm so sorry,' Carrie said softly. 'I know how painful it is to lose a family member.'

'I was away from home when it happened, had just got my first job with an American company based in Seville. I offered immediately to come back and work in the business with my father again, but he was adamant that they could manage. They had Manuel and a lot of other family to help so I didn't press the point.'

'And now you wish you had,' Carrie guessed softly.

'Maybe I should. It would have proved that I had the passion for the land. Something that is important to Dad.' He shrugged, his eyes suddenly serious.

'And do you have the passion for the land?' Carrie asked curiously. 'Or are you just pretending for your father's sake?'

'Of course I care about the vineyard.' Max smiled at her. 'I always knew I'd come back one day. But I didn't expect to inherit the estate. That has meant a major change in the direction of my life. I won't pretend that giving up my career isn't going to be a wrench.'

Their food arrived. Carrie had ordered smoked duck breast salad, and it was beautifully presented and succulently tender. But she could honestly say that she might have been eating cardboard for all the interest she had in the food. All her attention was on Max.

One course followed another, but Carrie hardly noticed any of it. She was intent on their conversation. Max was an entertaining dinner companion. And as well as telling her about himself he subtly seemed able to draw her out in a way that she couldn't remember a man doing in a long time.

She found herself telling him about her mother dying when she was seven and how she had been sent to live with her father, a man she'd barely known. 'It took me ages to settle down. He was never the paternal type and his wife Donna was no better. They were both heavy drinkers and used to spend all their time either getting over a hangover or working up to the next one.' She shook her head. 'My only salvation was my half-brother Tony. We used to look out for each other.' She smiled.

'You miss him a lot, don't you?' Max said gently.

She nodded. 'He was my best friend as well as my brother.'

Max reached across the table and caught hold of her hand. The firm touch was reassuring. 'At least you've got Molly.'

'Yes...' Carrie smiled. 'Thanks to you. Carmel thinks you are wonderful.'

'It's the Spanish charm, works every time.' Max grinned.

Carrie suddenly became conscious of his hand which was still resting on hers, and as her emotions turned from sadness to awareness her skin seemed to burn from the contact and tingling, responsive sensations seemed to rush through her body like an adrenalin overload.

Hurriedly she pulled away from him. 'Anyway, this is all very pleasant, but we haven't discussed work yet, have we?' she said, trying desperately to pull her mind away from dangerous emotions. 'You said you had some problems you wanted to discuss about the advertising contract.'

'I did, didn't I?' Max paused. 'But I read through it again today and everything seems to be in order.'

'Really?' She frowned.

'I'll sign it and bring it into your office tomorrow,' he said easily. 'When do you think we can start shooting the commercial for TV? I'd like to get that underway as soon as possible.'

'We'll start this week. I'll get onto it as soon as you bring me the contract.'

A waiter arrived to clear their dishes and ask if they would like coffee.

Carrie glanced at her watch. She could have lingered talking to Max all night but she felt that she should get back. 'I'd better get home, check on Molly,' she said to Max.

The waiter left them. 'I'm sure Molly is fine. Otherwise Carmel would have phoned.'

'Yes, but, even so, it is getting late and you have a long drive ahead of you back to the vineyard.'

Max shook his head. 'I have an apartment here in town that I keep for business purposes. I'll stay there tonight.'

'Oh, I see.'

'Come back with me if you want. I'll make you coffee. It's not far from here.'

The sudden invitation made her blood pressure soar. Going back to his apartment for coffee sounded like danger with a capital D. Yet she was profoundly tempted to accept.

Before she could say anything, however, a man in a white chef's uniform interrupted them. 'Hello, Ambrosio.' Max stood up immediately and the two greeted each other warmly before Max turned to introduce her to his cousin.

He was about the same age as Max, but there the similarity ended. Ambrosio was a lot shorter and stouter than Max. But he had the same attractive dark eyes and they seemed to sparkle with merriment as he spoke to them.

The two men seemed to be good friends; Carrie noticed the warmth of Max's conversation, the easy comradeship.

Estelle came over to join in and she slipped into the seat that Max had just vacated. 'Did you enjoy your meal?' she asked Carrie.

'It was lovely, thank you.' There was something about this woman that she didn't like, Carrie decided suddenly—something that made her feel wary. The idea bothered her because she couldn't say what it was, and Estelle seemed perfectly polite and friendly, which made Carrie feel a bit guilty for thinking such a thing.

'Max is lovely, isn't he? We all adore him.' Estelle lowered her tone and leaned a little closer over the table. 'You two seem to be getting on very well.'

'Yes, we are.' Carrie smiled as she remembered Max had told her that this woman was a gossip. Maybe that was why she felt she needed to be cautious around her.

'But he's a bit of a heartbreaker. So be careful.' The words were accompanied by a smile that didn't quite reach Estelle's eyes.

'I'd be surprised if he hadn't broken a few hearts,' Carrie murmured lightly. 'He's very good-looking.'

'Yes, but between you and I he enjoys the thrill of the chase these days. So I'd play it cool if I were you.'

'Thanks, but I don't need the guidance.' Carrie kept her smile firmly in place as well, but she didn't like the advice. It sounded a bit like a warning-off. 'We are doing just fine.'

'I'm so sorry; I didn't mean to sound interfering.' Estelle immediately sounded contrite. 'I suppose I worry a bit about Max and all these affairs he has. So do his parents. He's never really got over Natasha, you know.' She leaned even further across the table in a confiding way. 'She's back in town,' she said in a low whisper. 'Came in here for dinner last week.'

'Really.' Who the hell was Natasha? Carrie wondered. Was she his former fiancée? She glanced up at Max, hoping he would come back to the table and bail her out of this conversation, but he was still deep in dialogue with Ambrosio.

'Yes, really.' Estelle didn't seem one bit chastened by Carrie's flat tone. 'As for taking over the family vineyard, I don't think Max will want to stay around there for too long; he's used to his freedom now. And—'

'Actually you are very wrong about that,' Carrie cut across her firmly. This conversation had gone quite far enough. And if she were to play her part as Max's 'fiancée' she needed to put a halt to Estelle's ramblings.

'What do you mean?' Estelle looked at her blankly.

'I mean that Max and I are more than just getting on well together. And I think he is more than ready to settle down at the vineyard.'

'You mean Max is serious…about you?' There was disbelief, even a hint of scorn in the question as the woman's eyes raked over her with brazen contempt.

The unguarded moment of animosity made Carrie realise she had been right to be wary of this woman. Luckily she was saved from having to say anything further because Ambrosio interrupted them. 'I'm having to rush back to my kitchen, Carrie; it was nice meeting you.'

'And you.' Carrie got to her feet, glad to be getting away from Estelle. How did such a nice man get such an unpleasant wife? she wondered.

'Everything okay?' Max asked her as they stepped outside the restaurant.

'Yes. It was a lovely meal, thank you.' She was quiet as they walked back through the busy streets.

Snippets of Estelle's words played through her mind. 'He's a bit of a heartbreaker...be careful. He enjoys the thrill of the chase these days. So I'd play it cool if I were you.'

A busker was playing a romantic ballad outside one of the shops and she noticed that Max threw some coins in his hat as they passed.

'Who is Natasha?' she asked Max abruptly as they reached his car.

Their eyes met over the roof of the vehicle. 'I take it Estelle has been giving full vent to her theories about my love life?' he said dryly.

Carrie nodded. 'I had to dive in and tell her that we were serious about each other. I had no choice—she was saying that she didn't think you would ever settle down at the vineyard. And if the story of our engagement is to be believed I had to say something.'

Max nodded. 'You did the right thing.'

'Maybe...but after the shock faded from her expression I don't think she believed me.'

'Sounds about right.' Max's voice was grim. 'Don't worry about Estelle; she's difficult at the best of times.'

'I'm not worried,' Carrie said with a shrug. And she wasn't worried—she was annoyed. Annoyed because he still hadn't told her who Natasha was. When they had agreed on this charade he had insisted on knowing her background and if any of her boyfriends were likely to appear on the scene. Surely he should grant her the same consideration.

They got into the car. 'So, how about coffee at my apartment?' Max asked her lightly.

'No. I need to get back, Max.' There was no prevarication in her tone. Maybe earlier she had been tempted at the thought of being alone with him for a bit longer, but she had been firmly pulled back to her senses. They needed to be businesslike about this arrangement otherwise it could blow up in their faces.

He didn't try to persuade her, just nodded and started the engine.

So who was Natasha? Carrie wondered again as Max pulled out into the traffic. Was she the woman that Max had once spoken about so wistfully? The girl he had been engaged to?

She remembered the dramatic way Estelle had whispered across the table at her. *'He's never really got over Natasha.'* Before adding casually, *'She's back in town.'*

Maybe Estelle was right. Because if Max was over her surely he would have had no difficulty opening up and talking about her now, letting Carrie know the exact situation between them. If the woman was *back in town*, as Estelle had told her so dramatically, did that mean Max would see her again?

A curl of jealousy stirred forcefully inside Carrie. The feeling took her completely by surprise and horrified her. Why should she be jealous? Max's love-life was nothing to do with her. She couldn't care less.

Carrie bit down on her lip. She was probably tired. It was probably the strain of all these lies she had to tell. She hated lying. Yes, that was it. Of course she wasn't jealous. After Martin she had promised herself she would never feel like that over a man again and she intended to stick to that promise.

Max pulled up outside her apartment.

'Thanks again for a lovely evening.' She couldn't wait to get away from him now.

'You're welcome.'

She hardly even waited for him to finish speaking before she was reaching for the door handle. 'See you to-morrow at the office.'

To her surprise Max also got out of the car. 'I'll walk you to your door,' he said.

'There's no need.'

'Maybe not, but I'd still like to see you safely inside.' He locked his car and then moved to follow her towards the front door of the building.

The man was really irritating, Carrie thought as she struggled to find her keys. Why couldn't he just go away when she told him to? She was conscious of his closeness as she unlocked the door, conscious of the scent of his aftershave in the warm evening air.

As she pushed the door open he stepped inside with her, obviously intent on walking all the way up to the front door of her apartment.

'I'm okay now, Max,' she said, turning to look up at him. 'I can go up to the apartment on my own.'

'Are you angry with me, Carrie?' he asked softly.

'No! Why should I be angry?' Her heart started to pound against her chest as he moved a step closer.

'I don't know. Maybe it was something Estelle said.' The quietness of his voice in the empty hallway seemed to echo strangely. 'Or maybe you are scared of being alone with me?'

'That's ridiculous. I'm not scared of you—why should I be scared of you?'

'I don't know.' He reached and touched her face gently. It was a curiously tender gesture and it made her heart ache with a heaviness she couldn't begin to understand. 'Sometimes you look at me with a wariness that makes me think someone has really hurt you in the past...that you are scared of getting too close to a man again.'

Carrie was horrified by the observation. 'If I'm wary

of you then it's because you are a business client and this
charade is wrong. We are lying to people.' She hissed the
words in a low tone. 'Of course I'm uncomfortable.' She
swung away from him before he could continue with the
conversation and made her way upstairs to her front door.

He followed her. Carrie was appalled at how her hands
trembled as she tried to put her key in her door. He
reached past her and took the key from her hands to insert
it in the lock. The touch of his skin against hers made her
body start to pump with adrenalin.

'There, you see, you did need me to walk you upstairs
after all.' His voice was gently teasing. 'Now, are you
going to tell me why you are annoyed with me? What did
Estelle say to you?'

'She talked a lot of rubbish—'

'She usually does.' He stepped inside the narrow hallway of her apartment and closed the door. 'So what kind
of garbage did she spout this evening?' He seemed far too
close in the confined space and she backed away, only to
find herself up against the wall.

He put his hands either side of her head, leaning on the
wall and trapping her in the circle of his arms without
actually touching her.

His closeness made her senses reel. 'She didn't say anything that upset me. I just didn't like lying—maybe it
comes easy to you, but not to me.' Carrie whispered the
words fiercely, mindful that Molly's grandparents were in
the apartment. 'And I think you should have told me about
Natasha, and what she means to you. I didn't know who
Estelle was talking about.'

'Ah, I see.'

The ambiguous reply made her temper rise again. 'So
who is she?'

'Are you jealous, Carrie?' He asked the question very quietly and yet there was a serious underlying tone.

'Certainly not!' She swallowed hard on a sudden knot of panic in her throat. 'I couldn't care less; you can date who you want. I'm not in the slightest bit interested in your romantic dalliances. You may think you are God's gift to women, Max, but I'm not one of your blind admirers.'

'Is that so?' His voice held an edge of displeasure now.

Good—he deserved to have that male ego of his taken down a peg or two, she thought.

'Maybe women throw themselves at you wherever you go, but I'm not turned on by you in the slightest.'

'You didn't object too much when I kissed you, as I recall,' Max said wryly.

Carrie was furious that he had brought that up. 'Well, we were just playing a part. It didn't mean anything! In fact if you were any kind of gentleman you wouldn't stoop so low as to even mention that…incident.'

'Oh, I can stoop quite low when I want.' Max's voice was nonchalant and unconcerned.

Then before she realised his intention he bent his head closer and his lips found hers.

The shock of his kiss seemed to somersault through her body. Carrie clenched her hands at her sides and tried to force herself not to kiss him back. But his lips were tender and skilled and they moved over hers with such gentleness that she felt the anger inside her starting to melt away, to be replaced with a much more powerful emotion.

Desire hit her like a fist, dissolving her mind into a mass of confusion. And suddenly she was kissing him back. Her arms seemed to move of their own volition to rest on his shoulders.

His kiss deepened, and from tenderness and gentle persuasion a fierce hunger started to burn between them.

She felt his hands moving to span her waist; the touch of his skin seemed to burn through her dress. She wanted him, she thought fiercely. She really wanted him. The need was crazy and wild but it wouldn't go away. She wanted to feel his hands against her naked skin, touching her without the encumbrance of clothing.

When he pulled away from her she was shaking inside.

'There,' he murmured, a hint of pleasure in his tone. 'You see, you are not as immune to me as you like to pretend.'

The arrogant words made her blood pressure soar.

'And, just for the record, Natasha is my former fiancée. She is now married to someone else, so she will be no hindrance to our arrangement.'

Before Carrie could draw herself together to make any kind of reply he pulled away from her.

'Goodnight, Carrie, sweet dreams.'

Then the door closed behind him quietly, and he was gone.

She pressed her fingers against her lips. They still seemed to burn from the heat of desire, and she was still trembling inside with need.

CHAPTER SIX

THE Monday morning meeting was always stressful—
everyone sitting around the boardroom table vying for
José's attention, trying to outwit and outmanoeuvre each
other by coming up with bigger and better ideas for pro-
moting clients' products.

Usually Carrie was in there, fighting her corner. She
could think fast when under pressure, and she always did
her research and her homework well. It was how she had
won a lot of contracts each week. But this morning she
really didn't have the inclination to join in with the battle
of wits. In fact as she sat at the table and listened to the
raised voices and the constant backstabbing she found herself thinking how pathetic the whole war of words was.

Did it really matter that Mel's idea for the soap powder
company didn't sound as zany as the idea Gustavo had
come up with? It was hardly of earth-shattering impor-
tance. And who knew? Maybe the public would like Mel's
idea. Maybe the public were tired of zany ideas.

Carrie listened as José ruthlessly tore into Mel's work,
making her feel about two inches high. She could see Mel
was getting increasingly upset but José didn't seem to
notice; he was preaching the policy of *Images* with all the
vengeance of a zealous minister chastising a total sinner.

He was getting very worked up about nothing, Carrie
thought angrily. What mattered was that Molly's nanny,
Silvia, had come back to work this morning and had
handed in her notice.

'I must leave in two weeks,' she had said firmly when

Carrie had asked her to stay to the end of the month. 'My boyfriend is going back to Granada and he has asked me to go with him.' Joy had radiated from the girl's eyes. The contrast between her red-rimmed eyes and tear-stained face last week and the way she had looked this morning had been remarkable.

Love had a lot to answer for, Carrie thought grimly. She hoped things worked out for Silvia, because that boyfriend of hers had been letting her down for months. He didn't seem the reliable type at all.

But that was Silvia's problem, and meanwhile she was left with the dilemma of having no child-cover in two weeks.

It was a shame as well, because Molly had really liked Silvia, had got used to her. It was another change in her small life that she didn't need.

'How are things going with the Santos contract?' José asked her suddenly, his voice booming down the table, breaking into her thoughts.

'It's all under control, José,' she said confidently. 'Max Santos is signing the contract today.'

'I thought you said he'd sign on Friday?'

'It will be on my desk today,' Carrie reiterated. 'I'm organising a camera crew to get up to the vineyard this week because Max is keen to get things started straight away.'

José looked sceptical.

She hoped that Max *would* bring the contract in today. That he wouldn't start to play games.

For a moment the memory of the way Max had kissed her last night flashed vividly into her mind. The heat and the passion and the need he had stirred up inside her were still shockingly intense. Max had merely been proving a point because she had mocked him. But what was her excuse? How was she going to face him today?

'Okay, well, that brings our meeting to a close,' José said briskly, and immediately everyone started to tidy away their portfolios to get back to their offices.

'Hold on a moment, Carrie,' José said as she made to join the exodus.

She stopped beside him at the head of the table, and watched as he slowly put his notes back inside the folder in front of him.

'How can I help you, José?' she asked, trying to hurry him up. There were telephone calls she needed to make and a stack of paperwork waiting for her on her desk.

Even so, José waited until the last person from the meeting had gone out through the door before straightening and looking her in the eye.

'I just wondered how things were going with your adoption plans for Molly?'

'Things are going well. It's all going ahead.'

She saw the glitter of disappointment in his eyes. 'So Molly's grandmother isn't going to take her?'

'Molly is happy with me; her grandmother sees that.'

José shook his head. 'You are making such a mistake, Carrie. You have so much talent…so much going for you. Why tie yourself down with someone else's child? You are throwing it all away.'

'I'm not throwing anything away,' Carrie replied firmly. 'I love Molly and I can do my job and look after her as well. Millions of single mothers have successful careers—'

'You're throwing away our relationship,' José cut across her.

To Carrie's surprise he moved closer, and there was an expression on his handsome face that caught her off guard. 'I miss you,' he said gruffly. 'I miss our drinks after work...our dinners. Our closeness...'

'José, our relationship is over,' she said softly. 'It was probably a mistake to start with. We work well together and we should never have compromised that. Things are better left as they are now.'

José reached out and put a hand on her shoulder. 'I think you are wrong. I think we could have been a perfect team.'

It was strange how his hand touching her made no difference to her heartbeat, made little impact on her senses. She couldn't help comparing the effect he had on her with the effect Max had. The wild fluttering in her stomach, the heat and the desire that instantly sprang to life as soon as Max even looked at her.

'Carrie, please think about what we had. What we could have together,' José murmured. He seemed to be leaning closer; she thought he was going to kiss her. Panic-stricken, she made to step back from him and at the same time the door into the boardroom opened.

The intrusion took them both by surprise. And when Carrie saw that it was Max who stood in the open doorway her heart seemed to go into overdrive.

She noticed the way his dark eyes took in the closeness of their stance. But what he made of the situation was not clear; his features were impassive, his voice, when he spoke, cool. 'Your secretary told me I would find you in here.'

'Max, I didn't expect you until this afternoon.' Carrie didn't know why she felt awkward, but she did. All right, José had been standing a little too close to her for a discussion about work, but it was none of Max's business anyway. 'José, this is Max Santos of Santos Wines. Max, my boss, José.' She introduced the men swiftly, trying to regain her composure.

José was immediately his usual gushing, businesslike self as he stepped forward to shake hands. 'Good to meet you. We are very excited about the Santos project...very excited. I think it is going to be extremely successful.'

'Let's hope so.' By contrast Max's voice was steadily impassive.

'Well, you've got one of our best people. Carrie is extremely talented...we have the utmost faith in her abilities here at *Images*.'

Carrie wanted José to shut up; he was starting to sound like a very bad commercial himself.

'I've already discovered how special Carrie is,' Max drawled as the man paused to take a breath. 'Haven't I, *querida*?' He used the Spanish endearment for darling with nonchalant ease.

Carrie could feel herself starting to blush as both men's eyes were trained on her face. Max looked relaxed; José looked dumbfounded.

'I take it you haven't told José about us?' Max murmured, and then smiled at her as she blushed an even deeper shade of red. 'But I suppose you are right, business should be strictly business, so back to the matter in hand. I have our contract here—' he held up the folder '—but we need to talk over a few things. I thought we'd sort them out over lunch.'

Carrie's eyes narrowed on Max's face. She was furious that he had mentioned anything about their personal involvement in front of José. It was totally unnecessary and he was obviously playing some kind of game, because she remembered perfectly well that he had said the contract was fine over dinner last night. She wanted to contradict him, remind him of this, tell him they had nothing to discuss, but she didn't dare have a confrontation in front of José.

'Let's talk in my office, shall we?' she said instead, planting a brightly confident smile on her face. 'Excuse us, José.'

'Of course.' José stood back to allow them both to exit the boardroom before him. He still looked slightly shell-shocked. Max, on the other hand, looked so calmly self-assured that it was galling.

As soon as they had entered the private domain of her office Carrie closed the door and rounded on him. 'What on earth was that all about?' she asked angrily. 'Why did you tell José that we are involved personally?'

'Because we are,' Max answered calmly. 'Unless you've changed your mind about our agreement...' his tone suddenly held a hard edge '...and in that case I will have to rethink a few things.'

'What do you mean?' Carrie frowned. 'Look, Max, our fake engagement is in our private life...nothing to do with work. You had no right to tell José that we are seeing each other.'

'On the contrary, I have every right.' His voice was cold. 'You entered into an agreement with me. We are involved whether you like it or not.'

'Not during office hours—'

'So it's all right if I ring Carmel and Bob during office hours to tell them this is all a charade?' He watched how her skin suddenly blanched at that remark. 'You can't have it all your own way, Carrie.' The softly spoken words belied the steely glint in his dark eyes. 'We've either got an agreement or we haven't.'

Carrie felt trapped suddenly. 'I still don't see why we had to tell José,' Her voice lacked fire now.

'This is a big city, Carrie, but it is surprising who

knows who. For instance, your secretary is a distant relation of my brother-in-law.'

'Is she?' Carrie frowned in consternation. 'I didn't know...does it matter?'

'Of course it matters. You know how people talk. Is she aware of the fact that you and José dated recently?'

'I don't think so...we were always discreet.' Carrie stared at him and she suddenly realised that as well as wanting her to play the part of his fiancée there was also a matter of pride at stake here for him. He didn't want a fiancée—even a fake fiancée—who could be accused of infidelity.

'I didn't think.' She swept her hand through her long blonde hair distractedly. 'I just thought that the fewer people we drew into this deception, the easier it would be when it came to untangling ourselves.'

'We'll think about untangling ourselves at a later date. Now, I know you said it was over...but are you still dating José?' Max's eyes seemed to be drilling into her very soul.

'No. I told you he couldn't accept that Molly was in my life.' She turned to look at him then, her eyes a clear, candid blue.

The way she looked at him tore at Max. He didn't doubt that she was telling the truth, but he knew that he had interrupted a private moment between them. Maybe even a passionate moment. Max had never thought of himself as the jealous type but he felt the emotion now, just as he had when he had walked into that boardroom a few minutes ago. It was a searing red-hot jolt coursing straight through him.

Angry with himself, he glanced at his watch. 'We need to sort out a few ground rules, I think. Have you got time for lunch?'

'Not really, I've got telephone calls to make and—'

'Make them later,' Max ordered.

Carrie paused and then, seeing the serious expression on his face, she nodded. 'Okay, but I've only got half an hour.'

'Fine. We'll go somewhere nearby.'

Her eyes moved to the folder in his hands. 'Did you sign the contract?'

The question irritated him. She was always so damn businesslike. 'Not yet.'

'You said you would!'

'We'll talk about it over lunch.' He smiled sardonically. 'Look on the bright side; it will salve that conscience of yours. You can legitimately say you are having a working lunch.'

She shook her head. 'You are razor-sharp, Max Santos.'

'Just like to keep one step ahead, that's all,' he murmured.

Max watched as she sorted a few things out on her desk and gathered up her bag. He liked the way she moved; he liked the graceful lines of her body beneath the pale blue dress. Suddenly he was remembering the way she had responded to his kiss last night. The heat of their passion had been heavily intoxicating. He had wanted to take things further. It had been a wrench to move away from her, but he had forced himself to move back because he had told himself that things needed to be taken slowly.

Now he wasn't so sure that taking things at a restrained pace was such a good idea.

'I want you to come out to the vineyard next weekend,' he said abruptly as they made their way out towards the lifts.

She looked over at him, startled by the invitation. 'Why?'

The lift doors opened and he waited until they had stepped inside and the doors had closed before answering her.

'There is a family party on Sunday afternoon for the twins' birthday. I think you should be there—it will lend more credibility to our relationship.'

'I thought you wanted to wait a while before introducing me to your family? Didn't you say you wanted them to ask about me first?'

'They have already asked,' he said casually. 'I think Estelle was on the phone to my mother as soon as we left the restaurant last night. So we can move on to the next stage now.'

The words caused more than a flicker of disquiet to stir inside Carrie. Max, on the other hand, seemed perfectly at ease. This wasn't causing him a second thought. As far as he was concerned this was phase two of a business project—nothing more. She glanced across at him, noting how assured he was. How attractive. And then she found herself remembering the way he had kissed her last night and the desire that had plundered through her body like an invading army. It still hadn't abated and here in the close confines of the lift she could still feel its presence taunting her. The knowledge made her want to run as far away from Max Santos as she could get. It terrified her. How could she feel like this about someone who saw her as nothing more than a co-conspirator in a web of deceit?

'When you say next stage—' she asked the question tentatively '—what exactly do you mean?'

'Just what I said. You'll meet my family and spend the weekend with me at the vineyard.'

'The weekend? You want me to spend the whole weekend with you?'

'Is that a problem?' Max asked calmly.

The lift doors opened, letting in a blast of hot air. But it was nothing compared to the heat inside Carrie. A problem! she thought feverishly. Spending an entire weekend in Max's company trying to pretend that she wasn't overwhelmingly attracted to him would be a complete nightmare.

'I can't, Max,' she said swiftly. 'I can't leave Molly for so long.' That at least was true.

'I don't expect you to leave Molly; you must bring her with you. She'll enjoy the party on Sunday. Belle and Emilio are only a little older than her and there will be lots of other children there.'

They stepped out onto the street, but Carrie was barely aware of the busy roads, the intense sunlight. All her concentration was on how to escape from this situation. But nothing presented itself to her; her brain seemed to be paralysed when it came to excuses for not spending time with him.

'Where will we sleep?' She asked the first question that came into her head and he smiled.

'My house has five bedrooms, Carrie,' he said. 'There is plenty of room.'

He took hold of her arm as they reached a busy intersection of the road. 'You can ask Carmel and Bob to accompany you, if you like. They said they'd like to see the vineyard.'

Carrie wasn't sure if that would make things better or worse. So she didn't answer straight away. Luckily Max's attention was taken up with crossing the road, and by the time they got to the other side he had moved the conversation on. 'So we need to sit down and just go over a few ground rules.'

'Yes, we do,' Carrie agreed fervently. Could one of the ground rules be that he didn't touch her? she wondered.

Not even lightly, as now, because her whole body responded far too strongly to any contact. But if she said something like that he'd probably guess how strongly she was attracted to him. Maybe he already knew, because she certainly hadn't acted with any restraint when they had kissed. The thought was mortifying. Max Santos was arrogant enough.

They went into a small tapas bar on the corner of the junction. It was charmingly traditional. Parma ham hung from hooks above a highly polished walnut counter, where an array of tempting dishes was laid out for people to select what they wanted. Because it was still a little early for the lunchtime rush there was only one other couple in the place, and they were sitting on high stools at the bar, leaning towards each other with rapt attention, a bottle of wine on the counter between them.

Max led the way across the marble floor to a table directly beneath an overhead fan.

'So what would you like?' he asked, looking around for the barman.

An escape clause, plus a little something to make me immune to you, Carrie thought as he glanced around and fixed her with dark, intensely sexy eyes. 'Just…just a coffee.'

'The food looks good in here,' he said. 'Have something else.'

'Max, I don't want anything.' She glanced at her watch. 'I shouldn't even be here. I need to get on with my work.'

'It's no wonder you are so thin,' Max murmured as the barman came over to take their order.

Did he think she was too thin? Carrie wondered, and then found herself speculating about what his real girlfriends looked like. What Natasha had looked like. Very curvaceous, probably, with legs all the way up to her armpits. She found herself wondering again what had happened between them to split them up. Maybe Max had indulged in an affair and been caught out? Maybe he even regretted it. Hence the wistful look in his eye and Estelle saying he had never really got over Natasha. Not that she cared, Carrie told herself sternly. It was none of her business.

'So, about these ground rules,' she prompted him in a no-nonsense tone as he fixed his attention back on her. 'I think you are right—we do need to decide exactly how we want to proceed. First I think we should set a time limit as to how long we are going to keep this charade up.' Carrie started to feel better as she talked about the situation in practical terms. 'Now, I'm not sure when Carmel and Bob are going home. They had a one-way ticket. I meant to ask them about it this morning, but another problem cropped up and it went out of my mind—'

'What kind of problem?' Max interrupted curiously.

'Molly's nanny gave in her notice; she wants to leave in two weeks.' She met Max's dark sympathetic gaze. 'It's nothing I can't handle. I'll just ring the agency and start interviewing straight away. But it has caused me concern; it's another change in Molly's life and she is so vulnerable at the moment.'

Max nodded. 'It's a difficult situation. Molly does need the reassurance of familiar faces and routine.'

'Yes.' His understanding made her forget their practical conversation about time limits and strategy. 'It crossed my mind this morning that I should take a sabbatical from work. Just until I have another nanny on board and I'm sure that Molly is happy.'

'Would José give you time off?'

'I don't know.' Carrie shrugged. 'I've already had my

allocation for this year, plus some extra time when my brother died.'

The barman arrived with their coffee, bringing Carrie's mind sharply back into focus. 'Anyway, you don't want to hear about that. That's my problem and I'll sort it out,' she said swiftly. 'What we need to decide now is how long we want to keep up this pretence of being a couple.'

Max shrugged. 'I don't think we should tie ourselves down to time just yet. What's more important is that we present a united front. I suggest we announce our engagement at the party on Sunday.'

The suggestion made Carrie's heart start to race as if she were in a marathon. 'Isn't it a little soon?'

He smiled. 'On the contrary, I think it's long overdue. After all, Carmel and Bob have known of your intention to marry me since the first day we met.'

Something about the teasing quality of his voice made her blush. 'That was different. I was backed into a corner and I never actually announced it in an official way.'

'Even so—' he shrugged '—why should we wait? All my family will be present on Sunday; it will be the perfect time.'

Carrie felt she was wading in quicksand. She swallowed hard. 'I have to tell you, Max, that I'm not feeling happy about all this. I'm sure they will suss us out. I mean, I'm probably not even your usual type.'

'Maybe that's just as well,' Max grated.

She noticed the glint of dry humour in his eyes and it irritated her intensely. She supposed by that he meant that he usually dated a more alluring 'eye candy' type of woman. Max Santos was so damn sure of himself that it was exasperating.

'For what it's worth, you're not my type either,' she found herself saying defensively.

'So who is your type, then?' One dark eyebrow rose sardonically. 'José?'

'José is a very attractive man.' For some reason she felt compelled to defend her boss; she supposed it was pride. Max Santos was too damned sure of himself.

'Just a pity he doesn't like children,' Max drawled scornfully.

Her face flushed with colour at that. She wished she had remained silent on the subject of José now. Of course Max was right. José was a bad example of her taste in men—but then Martin wasn't any better.

'Sorry, I shouldn't have said that,' Max said as he saw her eyes darken with pain.

She looked away from him. 'So are you going to sign that contract?' she asked, bringing the subject swiftly back to business.

Max noticed how she immediately hid behind her work. 'I don't know. Are you going to try and back out of our arrangement?' he countered.

Her eyes narrowed on his face. 'Are you trying to blackmail me into carrying on with this pretence?'

All colour drained from her face when he didn't answer her immediately. 'You are, aren't you?' Her voice shook with angry disbelief. 'That's what you meant in the office when you told me I could back out but you'd have to rethink a few things.'

'Blackmail is a bit of a strong word, Carrie.' He shrugged. 'But you can't blame me for protecting my interests. After all, I've fulfilled my part of the bargain, but it seems to me that you keep trying to wriggle out of your side of things.'

'I'm not trying to wriggle out of things. I'm just genuinely concerned that what we are doing is wrong...'

'From where I'm sitting that just looks like you are

trying to wriggle out of the agreement,' Max maintained calmly. 'You are either with me on this or we call the whole thing off. There can't be any half-measures.'

Carrie looked at the contract, then back at him. She was furious that he was stooping to this. 'You're bluffing, Max. You need that advertising; it will be invaluable to the vineyard—'

'Save me the sales pitch, Carrie,' he cut across her calmly. 'There are other advertising agencies.'

She sent him a fulminating glare from ice-blue eyes.

'So what is it to be?' he asked, totally unperturbed.

'You really are cold and calculating, aren't you, Max?' she spluttered indignantly.

He shrugged. 'Stop wasting time, Carrie. Are you in or out of the deal?'

She gritted her teeth. 'I've already said that I'm in.'

'Sorry, I can't hear you?'

'I said I'm in.' She knew damn well that he had heard her. The man was downright infuriating. 'Now, are you going to sign that contract?'

'Yes.' He picked it up. 'I'll sign it on Wednesday, when I take you out to dinner.'

'Wednesday?' She was livid. 'I want you to sign it right now.'

'Patience, *querida*.' He reached across and tipped her chin upwards, studying her face with a cool intensity. 'We will go out to dinner on Wednesday and gaze longingly into each other's eyes. And you will assure me once again of your dedication to our little arrangement. Then I will sign your contract.'

Carrie wrenched herself away from the touch of his hands, her heart thundering against her ribs. 'You are totally infuriating.'

'And you are even more beautiful when you are angry.' He smiled.

'I've had enough of this. I'm going back to work.' She stood up from the table.

'See you Wednesday, seven-thirty as usual.'

She was going to leave without answering, but he caught hold of her wrist. 'Carrie?' He looked up at her with forceful intent.

'Yes…see you Wednesday.'

He let her go, a small triumphant smile curving his lips as he watched her walk away.

CHAPTER SEVEN

How had she had got herself into this situation? Carrie wondered as she drove Carmel, Bob and Molly up to the vineyard on Saturday morning.

She hadn't intended to ask Molly's grandparents to come with them. In fact she had firmly decided it was a very bad idea and would just cause further complications. It was Max who had issued the invitation. He'd rung them directly at the hotel. And the first Carrie had known about it was when Carmel had rung her at the apartment, gushing with excitement about the trip.

'You shouldn't have invited them,' Carrie had complained sternly to Max when they had met for dinner on Wednesday night. 'I'd decided not to. It's just an added strain. Now we are going to have to keep up our pretence all the time, not just at your niece and nephew's party.'

Max had shrugged and been completely unconcerned. 'If you remember, one of the first things they asked me when we met was if they could come up to the vineyard and I said yes. I'm a man of my word, Carrie. I'm keeping my side of our bargain.'

Carrie's hands clenched on the steering wheel as she remembered those words. The man had an arrogant nerve to talk to her about honouring his side of the bargain, when he had practically resorted to blackmail to get her to carry on with the arrangement.

At least on Wednesday night he had finally signed the advertising contract, she tried to pacify herself, which was one less worry. But he should never have invited Carmel and Bob to his home.

She could see all kinds of difficulties in the situation. Introducing Carmel and Bob to Max's mum and dad, for instance. That would be another step deeper into the quagmire of lies. She wondered suddenly if that was the reason Max had invited Molly's grandparents, as a kind of insurance policy. He knew with them around she had to maintain the lies perfectly.

She glanced into the rear-view mirror. Carmel was sitting in the back with Molly. She was singing 'The Wheels on the Bus Go Round and Round,' and Molly was giggling happily.

Everyone seemed happy; even Bob, sitting next to her in the passenger seat, kept smiling. He caught her glancing over at him. 'This is great, Carrie. The scenery is terrific out here.'

'Yes, it's pretty, isn't it?' Carrie glanced back at the road ahead. Guilt licked its way through her. Carmel and Bob were good people; she felt such a fraud. And Max's parents were probably equally nice.

How had she got herself into this? she asked herself for what seemed the millionth time. It was as if she had walked into a gentle breeze only to discover it was really a tumultuous whirlwind that had carried her away. She felt everything was out of her control and she was just being carried deeper and deeper into the epicentre of a storm.

She turned the car in through the gates to the vineyard.

'That's Max's house up ahead,' she said as the driveway curved and the white villa came into sight. It seemed to shimmer in the sunshine and the gardens around it were jewel-bright in the clear morning air.

It was as beautiful as she remembered, Carrie thought

as she brought the car to a halt by the front door. Hard to believe that it was just over a week since she had come out here for the first time; so much seemed to have happened since then.

The front door opened as they climbed out into the heat of the day and Max appeared. They hadn't seen each other since having dinner together on Wednesday, and her senses seemed to do a strange little leap as their eyes met.

Not that she was pleased to see him. How could she be pleased to see someone who was so coolly calculating? She remembered how they had parted on Wednesday night, how once again he had insisted on walking her up to her front door. How he had leaned closer to her as he whispered goodnight and she had closed her eyes, her senses in chaos. He had just kissed her casually on each cheek before pulling back. And strangely she had been disappointed. That had worried her…worried her enough to make this trip seem even more alarming.

Carrie wished she hadn't remembered that now as he came to greet her. He was wearing jeans and a white T-shirt. It was the first time she had seen him dressed so casually and it suited him, made him look younger, more boyishly handsome.

'Hello, *querida*.' She knew the husky endearment and the warm way he gazed deep into her eyes was for Carmel and Bob's benefit, but it still managed to make her emotions flutter with a dangerous energy. She felt shyly unsure as he put his hand on her shoulder and her adrenalin pumped wildly as she realised he was going to kiss her. This time it was no light kiss on the cheek; his lips touched hers with a firm possessiveness that made her senses spin. Then he was turning to welcome Carmel and Bob.

'Good to see you,' he said, shaking Bob's hand and

kissing Carmel on each cheek. 'Come on inside and make yourselves at home.'

As Molly came over towards him he crouched down to speak to her. 'Hello, young lady,' he said with a grin. 'How's Mojo today?'

Molly held the dog out for him to see.

'Is he looking forward to his weekend away?'

Molly nodded. 'He says he'd like ice cream for tea.'

'I shall put the order into the kitchen and you both shall have ice cream,' Max said seriously, and then grinned. 'Maybe even a double portion. But first do you want to see where you are going to sleep tonight?'

Molly nodded. 'Has it got a big bed?' she asked suddenly. 'I don't sleep in my cot any more.'

'It's got a bed fit for a princess,' Max said. 'You just wait and see.'

He was very good with her, Carrie thought as she busied herself getting their overnight bags out of the boot of the car.

Max came over to give her a hand. 'It's okay, I can manage,' she said, putting her lightweight bag over her shoulder.

'Always so independent,' he murmured, and then reached to take it from her anyway, and lifted Carmel and Bob's case up as well.

'Come on, let's get you all settled in and then we can have a drink,' he said resolutely.

Carrie watched the way Molly ran to keep up with him as they went into the house. She seemed fascinated by him. Even reached to take his free hand as they started to climb the stairs. She was surprised by the move; Molly was usually very shy around strangers and she had only met Max once before. Obviously Max's charms worked on old and young alike, she thought.

He showed Carmel and Bob to their room first. It was delightfully furnished with antiques, and the colour scheme of pale blue and white was restful and cool. 'This is lovely,' Carmel said appreciatively.

'There is a bathroom through here,' Max said, opening the door through to a luxurious modern bathroom that was cleverly and unobtrusively incorporated behind a row of fitted wardrobes.

'Anything you need, don't hesitate to ask. I'll leave you to settle in.' Max put their case down on the ottoman at the end of the bed.

Molly tugged on his sleeve. 'Is this my room?' she asked.

'No, yours is further down the hall.' Max smiled and took hold of her hand again. 'Come on, let's find it and see what you think.'

Molly's room had a plain white décor, but the bed was covered with a duvet featuring colourful cartoon characters. And toys and books lined the bedside tables.

Molly ran to investigate. She grinned at Carrie happily as she took one of the teddies down to look at.

'My sister gave me a few of the twins' belongings to make the room feel more homely for Molly,' Max explained as Carrie looked over at him.

'You've gone to a lot of trouble for one weekend.' She was touched by the thoughtful gesture. 'Thank you.'

'It was no trouble.' He moved to open a door that Carrie had assumed led into a bathroom, but instead it led through to an adjoining bedroom.

'This is my bedroom, Carrie,' he said. 'I thought it a good idea to put you in here because it has the adjoining room where Molly can sleep. That way if she wakes in the night you will hear her.'

Carrie followed him and stood in the doorway to the

room. It had polished wooden floors and a massive wooden four-poster bed with barley twist posts draped with white muslin curtains. This was Max's bedroom. The words seemed to echo inside her, and looking at the bed made butterflies dance in her stomach as if they were doing a wild flamenco. 'But where will you sleep?'

Max heard the hesitation in her tone. He turned and looked at her, a mocking smile on his face. 'What's the matter—frightened I might want to take our pretence a little too far?'

'No...of course not.' She felt her face starting to heat up. 'I...I just don't like the idea that you've had to get out of your room. That's all.'

'Well, if you feel too badly about it, I can always stay,' he drawled teasingly. 'I'm not averse to the idea. In fact, for appearances' sake we should be sharing this room.'

She knew she was colouring even more now; in fact she felt as if her whole body were on fire.

He grinned. 'Do you know? You look extremely sexy when you get embarrassed. Your cheekbones glow and your blue eyes seem to change to a deep midnight colour.'

'I'm not embarrassed,' she said quickly, trying to ignore the way his husky tone caused ripples of desire inside her. What on earth was wrong with her? she wondered angrily. Why was this man able to affect her so easily? 'I know you are only joking.'

'I'm not joking; people will expect us to be sharing a room. These are modern times...we are supposed to be engaged.'

'Well, I don't think Carmel and Bob are that modern,' she contradicted him heatedly.

'I think they are,' Max said firmly. 'We will have to at least pretend to be spending the night together...otherwise it will look odd.'

'Max, I—'

'Don't worry, I'll make sure they see me leaving your room first thing in the morning. That should suffice.'

'I wasn't worried,' she said, trying desperately to sound completely at ease. 'I think it's completely unnecessary.'

'Well, we don't want to cast doubt in Carmel's and Bob's minds about our relationship, do we?' Max said with a shrug. 'Attention to detail is important. After all, I'm a red-blooded male—you are my very attractive fiancée…'

She tried to ignore his teasing tone as she stepped over the threshold into his bedroom; she also tried to ignore a little voice that was asking her what it would be like to share this room with him, to lie in that double bed and be held in his arms.

The picture this conjured up in her mind caused her blood pressure to soar. To counteract it she tried to concentrate on the room and pretend he wasn't here…pretend that this was just a hotel bedroom.

There was little in the way of personal effects, she noticed. A few framed photographs on a desk against the wall were obviously of family members, and in the white *en suite* bathroom she could see there was some shaving gear and cologne on a shelf.

He put her bag down and sat down on the edge of the bed. 'We will have to run through a few details ready for the party tomorrow, whenever you are ready.'

'What kind of details?' she asked warily, wishing he wouldn't sit on the bed…wishing she weren't intensely tempted to sit beside him.

Maybe if she slept with him it would get rid of this burning curiosity and attraction she felt towards him? The idea crept into her mind, unwelcome and definitely unwanted.

She was so shocked by it that she hardly heard what he was saying next. Something about getting their stories straight.

Sleeping with Max Santos would be a mistake, she told herself forcefully. Okay, he was overwhelmingly attractive, and he could be extremely charming. But this was strictly a business arrangement, and she had witnessed at first hand how ruthless Max could be when it suited him. If she strayed from that reality into fantasy it could have very disastrous consequences. She had Molly to think about.

She crossed over towards the window and pretended to study the view. It looked out over a small grove of lemon and orange trees, and beyond that over the patchwork fields of the vineyard towards the distant purple mountains.

'They are bound to ask us questions about how we met. So we have to bear in mind what we have already told Carmel and Bob and stick as closely to the truth as possible,' Max continued. 'What do you think?'

'I think the truth is looking more and more like a very distant and alien planet,' she said unhappily.

Max got up from the bed and went to stand behind her.

He put a hand on her shoulder and forced her to turn around and look at him. 'Everything will be okay,' he said softly.

The gentleness of his tone didn't help to still the wild voices of desire that flared inside her just at the touch of his hand.

'I hope so.' She stepped abruptly away from him.

There was a strained atmosphere between them for a moment. Part of Carrie wanted to lean forward and put her arms around his neck, press her lips against his; she was shocked by the desire…horrified that she actively had to fight the temptation.

It was a relief when Molly came running in, a doll tucked under one arm and Mojo in the other. 'Auntie Carrie, can I keep this doll?' she asked very seriously, as if it were one of the most important questions of her life.

'You've got hundreds of dolls at home,' Carrie said with a smile. 'You don't need any more.'

'But I like this doll…' Molly's bottom lip started to wobble and Carrie suddenly realised she was overtired. She glanced at her watch. It was nearing midday…a little early for her siesta; usually Molly had a lie-down after her lunch. But Carrie was learning to recognise the signs, and she knew when she saw Molly rubbing at her eyes and looking fretful that if she didn't put her down for a sleep now she would have a very cross little girl on her hands in a few minutes. 'We'll talk about it after you've had a little sleep,' she said, moving away from Max. She picked the little girl up to give her a kiss. 'How's that?'

Molly hesitated and then nodded. 'Can I take the doll to bed with me?' she asked tremulously.

'Of course you can.'

Max watched as Carrie moved through to the other room and sat down with her on the bed. Listened as she gently persuaded her that her sandals had to come off before she could get into bed.

'But I don't want to take my dress off…or my shoes.' Molly was firmly against the idea.

'You can leave the dress if you must…but the shoes have to come off. A princess doesn't wear her sandals in bed. How silly would that be?'

Max smiled. He liked the way Carrie was so gentle with Molly…liked her understanding tone and the way she made the little girl laugh even when she was getting obstreperous.

He moved away from the window and went to stand in the open doorway through to the child's room. 'There is an air-conditioning switch by the door if you want to put it on, Carrie,' he told her. 'Or you can use the overhead fan.'

'I'll flick the fan on. I don't like air-conditioning—reminds me too much of the weather back in England.'

Max grinned at that.

Molly was climbing into bed now, and she pulled the covers up to her chin and then looked over the top of them mischievously. 'Will you read me a story?' she asked him.

'I'm going to read to you. Uncle Max is busy, Molly,' Carrie said.

'I'm not that busy,' Max contradicted her gently. 'Of course I'll read you a story, Molly.'

Molly gave a cheer. 'Can it be "The Owl and the Pussycat"?'

'I don't know. Have we got "The Owl and the Pussycat"?' Max asked Carrie.

She nodded, moved by the fact that he would bother to read to Molly. 'Yes, I've come prepared. But really, Max, you don't have to read, I'll do it—'

'Hey, I'm looking forward to "The Owl and the Pussycat",' Max said, a gleam of good humour in his dark eyes. She turned away and busied herself getting the books out of her handbag. There was a part of her that wished he would be useless around Molly, cool and aloof as José had been. Because the fact that he genuinely seemed to like Molly and was so good with her attracted Carrie to him all the more.

She handed the book across to him as he came to sit

in the chair at the other side of the bed. And then she moved to draw the curtains so that the sunlight was shut out of the room.

Max started to read as she made her way back to the bed. Molly listened with rapt attention. This was her favourite book. She asked for it to be read every day without fail. It was a wonder she didn't know it backwards by now, Carrie thought with a smile as she sat back down at the other side of the single bed.

She liked the way Max read the story, putting emphasis on certain words and making Molly smile. He had a wonderfully attractive voice, she thought. Her eyes moved over his face, taking the opportunity of studying him intently while he was otherwise occupied. His features were strongly handsome; there was a lot of power in the determined jut of his jaw. A lot of gentle humour in the dark eyes that from time to time glanced up at Molly. Her eyes moved to his lips. And suddenly she found herself thinking about how sensual they were…how wonderfully well they were able to ignite passion inside her.

I could fall for him in a big way, she thought suddenly. The notion hit her out of nowhere and with shocking intensity, and immediately she shied away from it. It was rubbish. How could she possibly fall in love with him? She had only just met him, for heaven's sake, and he was arrogant and forceful…look how he had threatened not to sign the advertising contract…that was a cold-blooded thing to do.

But the more she tried to deny the fact, the more the little voice inside her insisted that it was true.

He looked up and caught her watching him, and she realised suddenly that the story was finished.

'Again…again,' Molly demanded.

Max smiled at Carrie. It was a smile that seemed to

reach inside her and take hold of her heart to twist it slowly and unmercifully. And it made all those arguments about him being cold-blooded start to collapse…

'Read it again…' Molly said, trying to get their attention.

With difficulty Carrie broke the eye contact with Max. 'It's time for sleep,' she said softly to Molly.

'Just one more time,' Molly pleaded. 'Please.'

Max started to read the book again. Carrie tried not to look over at him; instead she watched Molly and told herself very forcefully that she was imagining things. Okay, she fancied him…she admitted the fact under extreme duress, but that was as far as it went. The idea that she was in love with him was just an illusion. It was all this play-acting, pretending to be a couple; it must have got into her psyche, and the fact that he was so good around Molly wasn't helping. That was all it was, just a case of getting carried away with an illusion.

Molly was obviously fighting sleep. Her dark lashes kept closing and then opening again as she tried to force herself to stay awake to listen to the story.

By the time Max had reached the middle pages the child was fast asleep.

'I think you can stop now,' Carrie whispered.

He looked over at Molly and smiled. 'She was very tired; obviously she's had a busy morning.'

'She was excited about coming here. So she went to bed later than usual last night.'

'How long do you think she'll sleep for?'

'She usually has about an hour.'

Max put the book down on the bedside table. 'Are you okay?' he asked her suddenly.

'Yes, I'm fine. Why?' She glanced over at him warily. She'd die if he had guessed what she had been thinking earlier. He'd probably be very amused...he was far too arrogantly confident to start with and she had her pride.

'You just looked a bit pale for a moment.'

'I'm fine,' Carrie reiterated, but her voice sounded false even to her own ears. 'Come on, let's get out of here.'

Together they crept out of the room, leaving the door ajar.

Once they were out of the darkened room and on the bright landing Carrie started to feel a little better. Maybe the intimacy of the bedroom had added to her delusional thoughts, she told herself. 'Thanks for reading that story to her,' she said briskly as they went downstairs. 'You are very patient with her.'

'I like children,' he admitted with a rueful grin. 'I suppose if I'm honest I'd like a little daughter of my own one day...'

Carrie glanced over at him, surprised by the revelation. Max had a lot of hidden depths, but that didn't change the fact that this was just a business arrangement. She was going to have to be very careful, she reminded herself firmly. Getting carried away by pretence would be stupid and extremely embarrassing.

Carmel and Bob appeared above them on the galleried landing. 'Where's Molly?' Carmel asked.

'Having a siesta.' Max was the one to answer. 'Come on down and we will have a drink out on the terrace.'

The sunlight reflecting on the turquoise water of the pool was dazzling as they stepped outside into the heat of the day. Carmel and Bob walked across the terrazzo patio and stood admiring the view. Carrie sat down under the shade of one of the huge parasols. 'Is it all right if I have a swim in the pool later today?' she asked Max as he took the chair opposite.

'Of course. You don't need to ask that, Carrie. I want

you to make yourself completely at home here.' He lowered his tone huskily. 'After all, we are to announce our engagement tomorrow.'

Carrie took a deep breath, trying not to think about that.

Max's housekeeper came out to ask them what they would like to drink. And Carmel and Bob came back to the table to join them.

The time seemed to fly by after that. Conversation was light and trivial and Carrie started to relax again. By the time lunch was served she was starting to think that really she was perfectly in control of this situation and that of course she could handle it.

'I must go and check on Molly,' she said, glancing at her watch. 'She'll be hungry when she wakes up.'

'It will be wonderful for Molly growing up here,' Carmel said suddenly before she got to her feet. 'Tony would be very pleased, Carrie. This would be everything he would have wished for her.'

Immediately Carrie's relaxed state disappeared, replaced by the heaviness of guilt. 'Yes, I suppose he would.' She carefully avoided Max's eyes across the table. And luckily Carmel and Bob didn't seem to notice her discomfiture.

'I remember he used to talk sometimes about how difficult his childhood was…and yours…and he always said that he would make sure that Molly never felt the way you did, that she would always have stability.'

'Yes, he did.' Carrie swallowed hard on a sudden knot in her throat.

'What are you going to do about your job when you and Max get married?' Carmel continued idly. 'Living here, you are too far away to commute into Barcelona every day, surely?'

'Well, I…' Carrie struggled to know what to say. She

could feel everyone's eyes resting on her, waiting for an answer.

'Carrie is thinking of taking a sabbatical from work for a short time.' Max came to her rescue. 'And then if she feels she wants to go back she might look for work nearer to home. There is a town about half an hour away from here that has a thriving business community. Maybe Carrie will set up her own advertising agency. She could install staff and come and go as she pleases.'

Carrie stared at him across the table. She had always thought that one day she might run her own busi-ness...hearing Max expounding such an idea felt really strange. But it was a fake description of a fake future together, she reminded herself quickly. And Max had to be a consummate liar to think it up with such impromptu ease. The accusation rested uneasily inside her; she hated it. And it was about then that she realised she'd rather believe the lies than think that about him.

'That's a good idea.' Carmel sounded pleased. 'And I suppose you will want children of your own before too long?'

Carrie didn't know how much more of this she could stand. She glanced over at Max and he smiled at her with the same warmth that he had upstairs over the bedtime story. 'That is a very real consideration, isn't it, *querida*?' he said softly. 'But I think we will wait until Molly is completely settled before we think about that.'

He seemed so genuine, so truthful... Carrie felt her grip on reality start to slip even further. There was definitely a part of her that was starting to wish that this weren't some hoax engagement, that this man was for real. She wanted to believe the gentleness of his smile, the tender-ness of his kiss.

Hurriedly she scraped her chair back from the table. 'Excuse me,' she said hastily. 'I must check on Molly.'

It was a relief to get away from the questions. Carrie practically ran up the stairs towards Molly's bedroom.

Her niece was still asleep. But Carrie sat down on the chair next to the bed to wait until she woke up.

Max wasn't the wonderful dream man that Carmel and Bob thought, she reminded herself forcefully. This was a charade. He was going to lie to his parents. All right, his motives were altruistic, but even so. It was still a lie.

Martin had been good at lying, she reminded herself suddenly. She remembered some of the elaborate tales he had spun, remembered how naively she had believed him. It was starting to look as if Max was the same type; he could certainly lie with the same effortless ease.

Molly stirred suddenly and opened her eyes. 'Hello, darling, did you have a good sleep?'

The child nodded and stretched.

'Are you ready for something to eat?'

'Where's Uncle Max?' Molly asked suddenly.

'He's downstairs. Come on, let's get you washed and changed and we can go down and see him.'

Having Molly around made the rest of the afternoon marginally easier. Carrie was able to keep busy helping her to eat some lunch and then watching over her as she ran and played beside the pool.

As the sun started to lower in the sky and the intense heat of the day lifted Max gave them all a tour of the vineyard.

'The soil around here is good,' he explained to Bob. 'And there is excellent drainage which means the roots at the vines push deep down to find the nutrients they need. Deep roots are important,' he added softly. 'It's the way the vines stay strong and healthy.'

'It's a bit like families…deep roots help keep them together and happy,' Carmel said with a grin.

'Exactly.' Max grinned back.

Carrie watched as he bent down and took a handful of the fertile soil before letting it slip through his fingers. Then he glanced up at her and their eyes connected for a moment.

'Deep roots are important…' The words played in her mind.

She watched Molly skipping ahead of them through the vineyard. The little girl seemed happier than she had in ages.

'When are you thinking of going back home to Australia?' Max asked them casually as he turned to lead them up towards the courtyard so he could give them a tour of the cellars.

Immediately Carrie wondered if he was asking so he could put a time limit on their phoney engagement.

Carmel shrugged. 'I don't know. We were thinking of just staying a few weeks. But of course if you were to set a date for the wedding that wasn't too far away we might consider staying longer. We have really nothing to rush back for.'

The words caused instant alarm inside Carrie. 'Oh, I don't think we will be rushing into anything, Carmel…I thought we already told you that.'

Carmel smiled. 'I know what you said, but it's very obvious that you two can't keep your hands or your eyes off each other. So why wait?'

The blatantly sensual words caused Carrie to miss her step and she stumbled slightly. Immediately Max put a hand out to steady her, but instead of letting her go he put the arm further around her and drew her in close against his body as they walked.

'That's very true, Carmel,' he said easily. 'Maybe we should think about setting a date; what do you think, *querida*?' He held her very tightly against him so that she couldn't pull away.

'I think we are not ready for that yet,' she said, her voice tight with anger that he was allowing this subject to continue.

'See what I'm up against, Carmel?' Max said, his voice lightly bantering. 'This girl's not easy to tie down.'

Carmel and Bob both laughed.

But Carrie wasn't laughing; she was furious at how easily Max was fooling everyone, and now he was making out that he was Mr Wonderful and she was the one dragging her feet over getting married…it was too much.

She supposed when their fake engagement broke up he'd be equally smooth at putting all the blame for their failed relationship onto her as well.

Maybe it was time to sow a few little seeds of doubt in Carmel's and Bob's minds about how wonderful Max really was. At least then it wouldn't come as a total shock to them when they heard the engagement was over…and they wouldn't automatically assume it was all her fault!

'I don't think you are being exactly fair, Max.' She spoke impulsively, without heeding any little warning voices, and pulled away from his arm. 'The reason we haven't set a date for the wedding isn't entirely my fault. You are equally to blame. You are so caught up with your work and worried about the vineyard that you've been putting off setting a date as well.' She glared at him. 'And you know it.'

There was a small silence. Bob and Carmel looked around at her in concern.

'He's making out that I'm the career-driven girl who is hesitating about making a commitment,' she told them, her voice shaking. 'And I won't have it because it's not true.' Carrie was surprised to find that the emotions raging inside her felt very real. She was still glaring at Max.

It was hard to tell what he made of her outburst. His dark features were impassive, his eyes serious and intense on her face.

As quickly as the anger had risen inside her it was diminishing again. What on earth was she doing? she wondered nervously. 'Anyway,' she said hurriedly, 'I just wanted you to know, Carmel and Bob, that it's not all my fault that we haven't set a date. Now, if you'll excuse me I'm going to take Molly back to the house.'

'Carrie, wait.' Max reached and caught hold of her arm as she made to turn away. 'You're right,' he said suddenly.

'I...I am?' Carrie looked up at him warily, wondering what on earth he was going to say.

'Of course you are. I have been worried about work and about the vineyard.'

'Yes, well, it doesn't matter now.' Hastily she tried to stop the conversation dead.

'Of course it matters.' He pulled her closer, his voice gentle, his eyes boring into hers. 'We'll set a date for the wedding this very week.'

Carrie's eyes widened in shocked surprise, and she was only vaguely aware of Carmel and Bob applauding wildly in the background.

'Do you know what you are saying?' Her voice rose unsteadily as she tried to warn him to back down before they were another step deeper into the jumble of lies. 'Now, Max, have you thought about this?'

He smiled. 'I've thought of nothing else since the day we met.'

CHAPTER EIGHT

CARRIE swam backwards and forwards down the length of the pool with forcefully energetic strokes. She couldn't believe how Max had turned the tables on her like that. What had he been thinking? The only explanation she could come up with was that he was determined he wasn't going to look like the bad guy when their relationship broke up.

Meanwhile they were now stuck with having to set a phoney date for a phoney wedding.

Carrie was so annoyed she had hardly been able to speak to him for the rest of the afternoon. And it hadn't helped when each time their eyes had met he had smiled as if everything were wonderful. This was all one big joke to him, she thought. Well, wait until she got him on his own. She was going to tell him exactly what she thought about his determination to seem like Mr Perfect.

Carrie stopped by the side of the pool and looked over the edge for her towelling wrap. The sun was very low now, and the encroaching darkness plus water in her eyes made it hard to see. She searched blindly with one hand, hoping to come into contact with the material, but it didn't seem to be there.

'Looking for this?' Max's voice took her by surprise.

She hoisted herself up a little to look across the patio. He was sitting at the table and he had her robe in his hands.

'Yes, I am. Will you bring it across for me, please?' Her voice was cool.

'Why don't you come and get it?'

The teasing question caused a violent stirring of disquiet inside her. What was he playing at? she wondered.

'Don't play games, Max,' she said crisply.

'You were the one playing games this afternoon,' he said quietly. 'Marvellous bit of acting, by the way. Congratulations.'

'Shh!' Carrie glanced towards the house. Carmel had volunteered to bath Molly and was upstairs with her now, and Bob was watching TV in the lounge, but even so voices could travel surprisingly far in the still quietness of the evening air.

'It's okay, the patio doors are closed.' He stood up and walked over towards her, but stopped a few steps away and held her robe out for her. 'It's safe to come out,' he said teasingly. 'I've already checked your body out several times with my laser eye and I assure you it's in wonderful shape.'

'You are outrageous!' she said angrily, and started to hoist herself out of the pool. 'And that stunt you played this afternoon was shameful.'

'You were the one who pulled the stunt.' He grinned. 'And pretty amazing it was too. A lovers' tiff…brilliant strategy. I think it gave a whole new feeling of reality to our relationship.'

'It wasn't a strategy,' she said through clenched teeth.

As she started to walk towards him the automatic lights came on around the side of the patio; they weren't bright but they were enough to make her feel as if she were suddenly standing under a spotlight.

She noticed the way his eyes raked over her figure in a way that was purely male and wholly admiring. His gaze moved slowly and thoroughly from the length of her legs, over the small span of her waist to the curve of her breasts in the yellow bikini. And disturbingly she felt an answering thrust of desire stir deep inside her.

'So if it wasn't a strategy, what was it?' he asked as she drew level with him.

She didn't answer him, but reached for her wrap instead. Infuriatingly he held it just out of her reach.

'Max, will you give me my robe?' she asked edgily.

'Not until you tell me exactly what was running through your mind this afternoon.'

'I think you know.' She glared at him. 'I was attempting to redress the balance between us. You realise, don't you, that the more you play the part of Mr Wonderful, the harder it will be for me when I have to tell Carmel and Bob that we have broken up? They are going to spend the future reminding me of how I let the most wonderful catch of the century slip through my fingers.'

'Are they?' He grinned. 'Well, that is gratifying to know.'

'You can take that smug look off your face, Max Santos,' she said crossly. 'Because I know the truth... remember...you are nothing but a fraud.'

'Did anyone ever tell you that you are even more beautiful when you are angry?' he said with a teasing grin.

'Don't try and change the subject, Max,' she said, trying desperately to hold on to all the sensible thoughts that should occupy her mind. 'Due to your sweeping remark this afternoon we are now going to have to make up some fake date for a fake wedding to satisfy Carmel and Bob.'

'We can do that,' he said nonchalantly. 'It's no problem.'

'It's a problem for me. You should have been a gentleman and taken the blame for a delayed wedding. Now Carmel and Bob are still going to be annoyed with me when I tell them a date that is a long way off.'

'Whatever date we choose to tell them they will just have to accept it.' He reached out and touched her face, tipping her chin up so that she was forced to look at him. 'So stop worrying.'

Desperately Carrie tried to hold on to the angry feelings that had fired her all afternoon. When she was angry with him it was easier to ignore the traitorous way her body seemed to respond to him.

'I don't think any of this is right,' she said shakily. 'You are a consummate liar, Max Santos. Just like my ex-husband—'

'Hey!' He cut across her swiftly. 'Before you get on your moral high horse, just remember that you are the one who started the lies. I bailed you out...remember?'

The reminder sat heavily inside her. 'Yes, but I didn't mean for things to go this far. And I was going to own up to Carmel when I bumped into you at the hotel.'

'But you didn't,' he said softly. 'What is that old saying..."Oh what a tangled web we weave when first we practise to deceive."'

'But my intention was to own up,' Carrie maintained firmly. 'You are just getting us deeper and deeper into this mess. You've even got Carmel and Bob believing that we can't keep our hands off each other, that there is a deep physical attraction between us...' She tilted her chin up and met his eyes defiantly, hoping that if she voiced the words decisively she could dismiss them. 'But that's just not true either.'

'Isn't it...?' Max's tone was seductively speculative. And then his eyes moved slowly down over her body again in a blatantly sensual appraisal.

Carrie felt as if he could see every inch of her skin in the wet swimsuit. She felt naked and vulnerable and yet in that instant more turned on than she had ever been in her life.

'Come on, Carrie, that's one thing we can't really lie about,' he murmured. 'There is a sexual chemistry between us and you know it.'

She felt her skin prickle with awareness as he leaned closer.

And before she realised his intention his lips captured hers. Softly provocative, they stirred feelings inside her that were smouldering with intensity.

Without thinking she moved closer and wrapped her arms up around his neck, her wet body pressed against his jeans and T-shirt.

When he pulled away from her she was shaking. Immediately he wrapped her robe around her shoulders.

'You're cold.' He rubbed the towelling material against her skin, his movements brisk to try and stop her shaking.

But she wasn't cold; she was shivering with pure need. She wanted him to touch her, to kiss her. The desire was eating her away and the contact of his hands moving briskly over her shoulders and her back was pure torture.

She couldn't take it any more, and moved closer again of her own volition.

'Maybe there is a sexual chemistry,' she admitted huskily. 'But that's all it is. Just sex. If we were to go to bed together the need would burn itself out. The feeling would die.'

'Do you want to put that to the test?' The question lingered, softly tormenting in the night air. 'Shall we make love and see where it leads us?'

Carrie's heart slammed against her ribs. She wanted to say yes so badly it hurt.

But before she could answer the patio doors slid open and she broke away from him hastily.

'Sorry to disturb you two lovebirds...' Carmel smiled '...but Molly wants you to tuck her into bed, Carrie.'

'Yes, of course.' Carrie moved swiftly away from Max, fervently glad of the excuse not to have to answer that question.

Tying the belt around her gown, she hurried into the house. What would she have said if Carmel hadn't interrupted them?

The feelings of desire had been so strong that there was a real possibility that she might have agreed.

It took ages to settle Molly down. She wanted Max to come and read her another story.

'Not tonight, Molly. You'll have to make do with me,' Carrie said firmly.

The little girl looked glum and folded her arms in front of her. 'I won't go to sleep,' she said. Then suddenly she said angrily, 'And I want my daddy.'

Carrie instantly put down the book and moved to sit on the edge of the bed. 'I know you do, darling.' She put her arms around her and drew her in close. 'I know.'

Suddenly she understood why Molly liked being around Max so much. Yes, he was good with her, but also Molly missed that male presence in her life. Her dad had worked from home; she was used to him always being around. She didn't remember her mother at all. It was Tony who had read to her, Tony who had played and joked with her. He'd been both mum and dad.

'Everything will be okay, Molly,' she said softly, stroking her curls back from her face. 'And we are going to a party tomorrow,' she said cheerfully. 'There will be lots of other children there; that will be fun, won't it?'

Molly nodded, and then she leaned back against the pillows. 'Will you read "The Owl and the Pussycat"?'

Carrie smiled at her. 'I'll read it twice…maybe three times if you settle down and try to go to sleep.'

In fact, Carrie had worn out 'The Owl and the Pussycat' and moved on to several backup stories before the little girl finally fell into an exhausted sleep. For a while she sat next to the bed, watching the sleeping child, wishing she could make things better for her. It broke her heart when Molly asked for her daddy…there was no easy way of dealing with it.

She looked over towards the chair where Max had sat earlier today. For some reason things seemed better when he was around.

Carrie remembered the way they had kissed by the pool, the heat of their passion, the need that had burnt so hungrily inside her.

'Shall we make love and see where it leads us?'

The question seared through her mind like a hot branding iron. Would it be so wrong to say yes?

A flash of light lit the room from the window. Carrie got up and went to look outside.

There was a storm brewing; she could see flashes of lightning far in the distance, illuminating the sky and the jagged outline of the mountains. Carrie pulled the curtains across, then walked back through to her own room.

She would have a shower and dress for dinner and she wouldn't think about what she should do; she would just take life a step at a time, she decided forcefully. Because all the planning in the world didn't seem to make much difference; events seemed to be carrying her along these days anyway.

Carrie had brought a pale buttercup-gold dress to wear for dinner. It was plain yet stylish and had narrow shoe-string straps that crossed over on her back, making it deliciously cool to wear. Something she was now very thankful for, because the heat of the night seemed clammy and intense due to the approaching storm.

She swept her hair up, away from her face, and secured it with some clips. Then, without bothering to analyse her appearance in the mirror, she headed out of the door. Her appearance wasn't important, she told herself as she went downstairs. This was just dinner…like any other meal she had shared with Max, and they weren't even alone. Carmel and Bob were here. There was nothing to be apprehensive about.

Yet as she turned towards the lounge and heard Max's voice she could feel her heart starting to beat its familiar rapid tattoo.

'Did Molly settle down?' Carmel asked her as she entered the room.

'Yes, eventually.' She smiled, wishing she weren't acutely conscious of Max's eyes on her. 'I hope I haven't kept you all waiting for dinner?'

'No, we were just having a pre-dinner drink,' Max said easily. 'What can I get you, Carrie?'

'Just a glass of wine, thank you,' she said, noticing the bottle of white open on the coffee-table.

She watched as he went across to pour her a glass. He was wearing grey trousers and a silver-grey shirt, and as always there was that effortless ease to his good looks, as if looking stylish just came naturally to him.

A bright flash of light outside made her look over towards the windows.

'Looks like there's an electrical storm heading our way,' Max remarked, following her gaze and watching as the sky lit up several times with jagged light. 'We get some spectacular storms sometimes.'

'I didn't think it would rain much around here at all,' Bob said as he got up from his chair to look outside.

'It doesn't, but when it does it can be violently tropical.'

There was a low rumble of thunder suddenly and it made Carrie jump.

'You're quite safe. It's miles away yet.' Max handed her the glass of wine and as their hands touched briefly she felt a force that was much more worrying than any storm outside.

The housekeeper came in to tell them that dinner was ready and she was pleased at the opportunity to turn away from Max. She didn't want him to see how the slightest look, the slightest touch, affected her. Maybe he was arrogantly used to women falling at his feet, but she didn't want to be just another one of his conquests. She had her pride.

The dining room looked magnificent. Four places were laid facing each other across the highly polished candlelit table and the doors out onto the terrace were open, giving a view of the floodlit pool and the storm that was playing dramatically over the mountains.

Max took the seat opposite her, and as she looked across at him he smiled. 'You look very beautiful tonight, *querida*,' he said softly.

'Thank you.' She smiled and tried not to look as if the compliment meant very much. But it did…and it wasn't just the words…it was the way he *said* them. The way he seemed to be able to look so deep into her eyes—into her soul.

A warm breeze ruffled the flames of the candles, making them flicker and dance. And again she found herself remembering his words earlier. *'Shall we make love and see where it leads us?'*

She remembered the thrill of his lips against hers, and the way she'd felt when he'd touched her body. If Carmel hadn't interrupted them she would have said yes to him...she had wanted him... Still wanted him.

Hastily she reached for her glass of wine, telling herself firmly that she should just be shrugging those feelings away as a moment of madness. There was a danger in feeling so passionate about a man...especially a man who was a fluent liar just like her ex-husband.

Lovemaking was probably just a game for him. Oh, yes, he'd kiss her, and if the opportunity presented itself he wouldn't hesitate to make love to her with fire and passion, but with no real feeling in his heart. And then when it suited him and this arrangement had outlived its usefulness he would calmly walk away without so much as a backward glance.

Carrie wasn't naive; she had learnt her lessons the hard way.

An appetiser of tiger prawns and crisp green salad was placed before her, and she tried to turn her attention away from her innermost thoughts and onto the conversation around her.

Bob and Max were discussing the wine business.

'There is more and more competition these days,' Max was saying casually. 'Award-winning wines have got to have a good sales base and market skills are very important. That's why I'm so pleased to have Carrie organising the advertising for us. She's come up with some brilliant ideas and it's the first major step towards modernising the vineyard.'

He smiled at Carrie as their eyes met briefly.

'You very nearly didn't use *Images* advertising services,' she said, remembering how he had deliberately held back from signing the contract...how he had threatened to go somewhere else. They were facts she had to keep firmly in her mind. 'You were almost going to go somewhere else.'

He smiled at that. 'I would never have gone anywhere else, Carrie,' he said softly.

'You mean you were bluffing?'

'Of course.'

Carrie held his gaze for a long moment, wondering if that was the truth or if he was just playing to the gallery.

He sat back in his chair, perfectly at ease. 'A man needs a few tricks up his sleeve when he is pursuing a beautiful woman.' He glanced over at Bob. 'Isn't that right, Bob?'

'Certainly is.' Bob laughed.

Max was definitely playing to the gallery, Carrie told herself crossly. Then he looked back at her and smiled and the element of doubt crept back in. When he smiled at her like that suddenly she wasn't sure of any-thing…even her own name.

The conversation centred on advertising for the vine-yard for a while. Usually Carrie would have joined in enthusiastically to discuss the project. But right at this moment she found that business was the last thing she wanted to talk about.

And suddenly she was wishing that Carmel and Bob weren't with them, that she could have Max all to herself. And what did it matter if a love affair between them didn't last? At least she would have enjoyed herself…life was short. They were both single; it wasn't as if they would be hurting anyone else by getting involved.

Carrie reached for her wine and took a gulp as she realised the dangerous direction her thoughts were taking.

The main course was served and the conversation moved from sales of wine to life in Australia.

'You and Carrie must bring Molly over for a family holiday some time,' Carmel told Max.

'We'd love to.' Max glanced over at Carrie. 'Wouldn't we, *querida*?'

A family holiday—the words had a pleasing ring to them. But they weren't a family and they never would be, she reminded herself sternly. From somewhere she managed to murmur a token acceptance. 'That's very kind of you, Carmel.'

The storm outside rumbled closer and Carrie looked out towards the terrace apprehensively.

'I take it you don't like electrical storms?' Max asked gently.

'I'm not scared of them,' she said quickly, then caught his eye and grinned. 'But, put it this way—if I was at home I'd be running around pulling out plugs now.'

He smiled. 'Don't worry, I'll look after you. If it comes any closer I'll plunge the place into darkness,' he promised.

Carrie looked across at him and smiled back.

Carmel and Bob were talking about the best time of year for a visit to their place, but the words seem to drift over Carrie. For a moment it seemed that everything narrowed in the room and it was just her and Max. Even the storm outside seemed to fade to oblivion.

Carrie found herself imagining what it would be like to go upstairs with him. She remembered again the way he had kissed her by the pool and the intense feeling of sensuality as her body had briefly touched against his. If he could turn her on like that just with a kiss, imagine what he could do if she threw caution away.

'Carrie…?' Someone's voice seemed to be coming from a long way away.

'Sorry?' She looked around and saw that the housekeeper had cleared their dishes away and was offering her coffee. 'Oh…yes. Thank you.'

Carmel smiled. 'I was just saying, if you don't mind I think Bob and I will skip coffee and turn in early. We are both exhausted, and Bob still hasn't recovered from the flight.'

'Oh! No, of course not,' Carrie said. She felt herself starting to burn with embarrassment as she realised she hadn't heard a word anyone had said because she had been too busy gazing into Max's eyes. 'I'm going to have an early night myself.'

'I thought you might,' Carmel said with a grin. Then laughed as she saw the disconcerted look on Carrie's face. 'Oh, don't worry, I'm a woman of the world,' she said, waving a hand in airy dismissal. 'And besides, you will be getting married soon. You two lovebirds enjoy yourselves.'

'Really, Carmel, you don't have to rush off on our account.' Carrie was mortified, and she didn't dare look across at Max to see what he made of this conversation.

Carmel laughed and pushed her chair back from the table. 'Anything past ten is a late night for us these days. No, if you will excuse us, we will retire. Thank you for a lovely day, Max.'

'You are very welcome,' Max said with genuine warmth. 'I've enjoyed your company.'

'Will you just put your head around the door and check on Molly for me?' Carrie asked as the couple headed for the door.

'Of course we will.' Carmel smiled at her reassuringly. 'See you in the morning.'

As the door closed behind the couple Max reached and topped up Carrie's wine glass. 'I told you Carmel was a modern woman,' he said with a grin.

Carrie felt herself heating up again. 'She was just being diplomatic because she thought she had embarrassed me.'

Max raised his glass towards hers. 'Anyway, I think it went very well this evening,' he said smoothly.

'Yes, they are a pleasant couple.'

'They are. And very understanding too.' Max grinned at her, a wickedly teasing glint in his dark eyes.

Instead of reaching for her wine, she took a sip of her coffee, hoping that the caffeine might help bring her back to her senses.

But as she looked across the table at Max the wild idea of how good it would feel to be in his arms persisted.

The candlelight flickered in a sudden breeze, casting dancing shadows across the table and over his features.

It was starting to rain outside now, and several wild flashes of light lit the night sky followed by a sudden roar of thunder that hung threateningly in the air.

Max leaned back and unplugged the lamp on the sideboard behind him, plunging the room into darkness except for the candlelight. 'Is that better?' he asked softly.

Carrie wasn't sure if it did make her feel better. The darkness that surrounded them now made the warm circle of candlelight enclosing them much more intimate. But she managed to smile coolly. 'Yes…much better.'

'If you'd like we can take the candles and our coffee into the lounge and make ourselves more comfortable?'

It seemed like such a logical invitation and yet the atmosphere between them was anything but.

'No, it's getting late.' Carrie dragged her eyes away from his with difficulty. 'It's been a lovely evening but I should really turn in myself.'

But the truth was she didn't want to leave now. It was very odd but something had happened over dinner…something that made her reluctant now to break the feeling of intimacy that danced between them in this golden circle of candlelight.

Telling herself firmly not to be so foolish, she tried to push her chair back from the table but she found she didn't want to move.

'Carrie?'

She looked over at him hesitantly.

'You know you've been driving me crazy ever since I set eyes on you...don't you?'

The huskiness of his tone seemed to tear into her consciousness. Her heart was beating with even greater force now. 'I...I think it would be a mistake for us to get fact and fantasy mixed up...' She said the words swiftly, as if by conjuring up sensible words it would break the spell of desire.

He reached out and took hold of her hand across the table, his thumb stroking across her skin. The gentle caress sent whispers of need shivering straight through her.

'But the fact is I want to make love to you...and I think...no, I know that you want me.'

His eyes were mesmerising; they made her feel almost light-headed with yearning. She found her eyes drawn to the softness of his lips as she remembered how good they had felt against hers.

'Maybe I do,' she murmured, completely lost now in the sensations that seemed to be drawing her closer and closer in towards him.

A smile of satisfaction curved his lips. She noted it and it made her temperature rise. 'But it doesn't mean anything,' she added hastily.

There was a moment's silence. A moment when the storm outside seemed to intensify, and the thunder roared as wild and as untamed as the beating of her heart.

Somehow she forced herself to get to her feet. He also stood up.

'Anyway, thank you for a lovely evening.' She was desperately trying to hang onto a shred of sanity.

He came around the side of the table. Then slowly but with deliberation he caught hold of her arm.

She looked up at him questioningly.

Then he lowered his head and kissed her.

His lips were gentle at first; they played with her in a tantalisingly provocative way that made her hungry for so much more.

The wild, untamed roar of thunder outside seemed to echo the feelings that were suddenly racing through her. Her hands curved up and around his neck as she moved even closer, loving the feeling of his arms wrapping around her, so strong...so passionate.

Their kiss deepened, his mouth exploring hers with a skill that shook her to her core. Sensations raced through her body, wild and frantic emotions that she had never experienced before.

She wanted this man. No, she more than wanted him— she craved him, she needed him—her whole body cried out for more.

Her breathing was ragged and uncontrolled as he pulled back slightly.

'I think we should continue this upstairs, don't you?' The quietly confident question should have restored some sense of sanity, but as she looked into his eyes she knew that the last thing in the world she wanted was to pull back from him now.

But at the same time she still wanted to hold onto her pride. 'You mean you think we should put my theory to the test?' she murmured huskily. 'Sate our desire and let this need we feel for each other burn itself out?' She angled her chin up so that her eyes could meet with his.

He reached out and touched her lips with his fingers,

stroking across them in a way that set all her senses racing wildly, wanting to feel his hands against her body.

Then he spoke to her in Spanish. *'Let's just take this one step at a time... one moment at a time.'*

Carrie's heart was thundering wildly as he took hold of her hand and turned to lead the way upstairs.

CHAPTER NINE

As MAX led Carrie into his bedroom he reached to put on the overhead light and she stopped him, putting her hand over his.

'Let's leave the light off, Max,' she whispered softly. Suddenly she was feeling extremely nervous. What was she doing? she wondered. Was she getting fact and fantasy mixed up in her mind? Because the fact was that her arrangement with Max was just a business pact; the engagement was nothing more than a sham. She hardly knew this man, and she had never indulged in casual sex in her life before.

Max did as she asked and left the light; instead he moved to close one of the windows, dulling the sound of the lashing rain. Although the room was in darkness it was lit every few moments by the sudden luminosity of the storm. It showed the surroundings in a succession of flickering pictures, revealing the four-poster bed swathed in its misty web of white gauze curtains.

'Are you okay?' Max turned to look over at her and she realised she hadn't moved a step from the door.

'Yes...but it's warm in here.' She felt as if she was burning up, but she didn't know if that was nerves or the actual temperature.

Max flicked on a switch beside the bed and a wooden fan on the ceiling started to whir, throwing out a deliciously cooling breeze.

'Is that better?' He moved towards her and she felt her heart starting to race again.

'Yes, much...' Her voice sounded huskily unsure.

'Are you having second thoughts about this?' He was so close to her now that she could feel his breath against her skin.

When she didn't answer him immediately he reached out and touched her face, tracing his fingertips gently over her skin, tracing the delicate heart-shaped contours and high cheekbones as if he were reading her using Braille. His touch was whisper-soft, yet it sent delicious shivery sensations shooting through her entire body.

'Carrie, have you changed your mind about this...?' He whispered the words as if he didn't want to say them but was forcing himself to hold back.

She looked up at him, and her doubts started to melt away, and suddenly this didn't feel wrong; suddenly it felt as if it was her destiny to be here with him in this room.

'No, I haven't changed my mind.' She stood on tiptoe and pressed her lips against his, tentatively at first, and then as he kissed her back with a deep, sweet gentleness passion ignited in a blaze of almost primitive heat. It was so incredibly strong that it made Carrie's senses reel.

His hands moved from her face down the slender column of her neck, then she felt his fingers on the buttons at the back of her dress. He unfastened them with ease, at the same time kissing her throat, her shoulders. Then he pushed the dress down so that it slithered to the floor, leaving her standing before him in just her lacy bra and pants.

He whispered huskily to her in Spanish, his fingers caressing the curves of her breasts, tracing the imprint of her nipples through the lace of her underwear. The sensation was unbearably erotic. She pressed herself closer to him with a fierce, hungry need, welcoming the touch of his hands, impatient for her underwear to be totally discarded and to feel his fingers against her naked flesh.

Carrie had never been so feverishly impatient for any man; her body and her senses were completely out of her control.

He captured her lips again, his tongue exploring her mouth now with a slow, masterful sensuality. She felt her stomach flip inside with wild excitement. Max's caresses were tormentingly slow, his responses measured to give maximum arousal, making her gasp even more with need. He was very much in command of the situation, playing with her as a panther might toy with its prey, enjoying the power he was able to exert over her.

His hand moved to span her waist, then moved to her lower back, running smoothly down to her bottom, caressing over the lace of her pants, feeling the smooth, firm curves of her body, pulling her in closer so that she was aware of just how much he wanted her.

The strength of his arousal made her heart dip wildly.

'Max, I want to feel you inside me.' Her voice when she found it was a low cry of need.

This wasn't a state she had ever been in before and she was totally bewildered by it. Disorientated by the strength of her emotions. She clung to him like a child as he picked her up to carry her to the bed. But as she felt the cool sheets beneath her back and felt his body covering hers she had never felt so womanly in all her life.

He pushed her bra to one side, taking her nipples into the warmth of his mouth, licking at the raised hardness. Carrie heard someone moaning and realised it was her... She had never made noises like that before; she tried to stop, but couldn't.

He was kissing her all over now, her shoulders, the flatness of her stomach. She writhed in ecstasy. Then he moved away. Pushing the net curtain on the bed back, he stood up. For an awful moment she thought he was leaving.

'Max?' She sat up slightly, pushing her blonde hair out of her eyes. Then saw that he was taking his clothes off. She watched him with greedy eyes, taking in the perfect proportions of his body. It was like watching a flickering film, as one moment he was in deep shadow, the next she could see him clearly in the white light from the storm.

He had a most fabulous physique, strong and lean, wide shoulders tapering down to narrow hips and a perfectly flat stomach. Carrie had never thought of a man's body being beautiful before, but his was. She couldn't take her eyes off him.

When he joined her on the bed again he smiled down at her and spoke in Spanish. *'You're beautiful, Carrie, so beautiful…'* The words made her stomach tighten with pure sexual need.

He kissed her full on the lips, slowly, with tantalising sweetness, reaching behind her to unhook her bra. So now she only wore her pants.

Then slowly, with deliberately teasing fingers, his hands stroked down over the lace of those pants before pulling them down.

'Tell me again that you want me…' The rough, husky command was made in a low growl that sent answering shivers of excitement rushing through her.

'I want you so much,' she answered him in Spanish and reached to touch him, and heard his gasp of pleasure.

Then his body moved to cover hers. The contact of his naked skin pressed against hers made her senses sing with pleasure. He laced his fingers through the silkiness of her hair and as he looked deep into her eyes his body took full possession of hers.

She gasped with the sudden shock of pure ecstasy. The feelings flooding through her body were wildly exhilarating and her body flexed and moulded against his. It felt as if this was so right, as if someone had designed their bodies to make a perfect fit.

Their hands laced together behind her head as he moved against her. It was as if they were dancing together, caught up in their own private world that matched the force of the thunderstorm that still roared outside with deafening might.

He whispered in Spanish against her ear, tormenting her with such ease, as if her cries of pleasure turned him on to even greater passion. Their movements became wilder and wilder; she was crying now, her whole being caught up in a tempest of desire that knew no bounds. Just when she knew that she could hold back no longer Max brought her to climax, coming with her in a fierce thrust of dominance that made her cry out.

Afterwards he cradled her to him, his strength turning to a tenderness that for some reason also felt unbearably erotic. Carrie had never felt so cherished, so safe in all her life as he held her against his chest. Such intense emotional joy after sex was wildly unexpected. Carrie didn't understand what was happening inside her and she didn't want to analyse it in any way in case she spoilt the moment. So she just curled up against him, enjoying the sweet peppering of kisses that he rained down on her face, neck and body.

As they lay entwined in each other's arms the rain still pounded down outside and the flashes of light still flickered through the room like the headlights of passing trains.

She slept so deeply and soundly that when she next opened her eyes she couldn't think where she was.

Early-morning sun streamed through the windows and there was the sound of complete silence from outside. Usually she could hear the distant roar of traffic when she lay in her bedroom at the flat and the tranquillity of the morning disconcerted her. Something was different.

It was only when she looked across at the empty space next to her that reality rushed back in, and with it vivid memories from the night before.

What on earth had she done? Carrie sat up in the bed and looked around the room, but she was on her own. Max had gone. Last night might all have been some crazy dream except for the fact that her dress lay in a rumpled heap on the floor, and wild recollections were flicking through her mind with searing clarity.

Carrie had never given herself so freely, so wantonly to a man before, and she couldn't understand what had happened to make her so needy…so *reckless*. Even when she had made love with her husband she hadn't felt such an overwhelming rush of complete need…had never been completely out of control…and she had thought she had loved Martin.

She leaned back against the pillows and put her hands over her eyes, trying to blot out the memories that blazed defiantly through her mind. The touch of Max's skin against hers, the taste of his lips; the way he had stroked and caressed her until she was begging for complete fulfilment. The mere recollection made her heat up inside; it also caused a rush of renewed longing…a wish that he were here beside her now.

So much for the hope that a night of passion might sate her desire, she thought angrily. It seemed to have had the opposite effect; it seemed to have increased her need for Max. And where was he? Probably he had stolen away as soon as she had fallen asleep, his desire satisfied. It had just been sex, nothing more, so why should he have stayed around and woken up with her?

She got out of bed, annoyed with herself for caring. Last night had just been a momentary aberration…and she wouldn't give it another thought, she told herself. Wrapping herself in her robe, she crossed to look through the doorway into Molly's bedroom. The child was still fast asleep; she might just have time to shower and dress before she woke.

Carrie headed quickly into the bathroom and turned on the shower. Then stepped under the forceful jet of water. As she soaped her body she tried not to think about the way Max's hands had caressed her all over last night.

She turned her face up to the warm water, allowing it to flow over her completely, as if it could wash away every trace of Max's hands and lips, every memory of how good it had felt to lie beside him. It had just been sex, that was all. It hadn't meant anything. These were modern times. People enjoyed a night of passion and didn't get hung up or embarrassed about it; they just forgot about it. Max would forget about it. She should do the same. Trouble was, she had never been completely at ease with that casual view of sex…had never indulged in a one-night stand in her life.

Yet last night she had given herself without any reservation to Max. She had held nothing back; her responses had been totally and utterly uninhibited.

So why had her behaviour been so out of character?

Then suddenly out of nowhere she was remembering the way he had held her after they had made love, that feeling of warmth and tenderness and being completely cherished. The memory was like an electric shock going through her.

Had that feeling been in her imagination? Probably.

After all, Max had told her categorically that he didn't want a serious relationship. In fact that was one of the pluses of their arrangement...*no strings*. He had specifically said those words to her. He liked the fact that she wasn't the type to get carried away with their deception.

So last night had definitely just been about sex. She squeezed her eyes tightly closed and told herself not to analyse what had happened between them any further, but to leave it under the category of enjoyable.

Instead she tried to concentrate on the day that lay ahead, meeting Max's parents and pretending to be madly in love with their son.

The prospect had seemed daunting yesterday, but today it took on an even more nerve-racking prospect.

She had never been any good at lying; everyone would look at her and they would know the truth.

They would look at her and they would know...that she was deeply, madly in love with Max. And that it was a love more intense, more staggeringly real than anything she had ever felt before.

The truth crept into her consciousness unexpectedly and quietly and caused Carrie to freeze with panic. She snapped off the shower and stood for a moment going over the words again.

I love him, she thought...I *really* love him.

The knowledge was mortifying, especially as she knew the score. Last night meant nothing to Max and this engagement also meant nothing. When her part of the bargain was fulfilled and his parents were happy their association would be finished. He would probably never even see her again.

The pain of that reality seared through her.

'Carrie?' Max's voice coming from the bedroom caused a flood of apprehension and emotion to race through her body. How was she going to face him with any kind of dignity? How was she going to hide her feelings and keep her pride intact?

'Carrie?' He was immediately outside the bathroom door now.

'Won't be a minute. I'm just getting out of the shower.' Hastily she stepped out and reached for a towel to wrap around her body. Her hands were shaking; in fact her whole body was shaking with reaction.

'I've brought you a cup of coffee.'

'Thanks, put it down on the table out there.' Carrie leaned back against the door and closed her eyes. 'Hey, if you are lucky you might bump into Carmel as you leave the bedroom. Add some more credence to our mock engagement.' She forced herself to sound light-hearted—but it took every ounce of self-possession.

'Maybe so.' He sounded nonchalantly indifferent. 'Are you going to come out and say good morning before I leave?'

Carrie hesitated. She knew she was going to have to face him at some point, but not now. Just say he guessed how she felt...? It was humiliating.

It was a relief when she heard the sound of Molly's footsteps running in towards the bedroom and her voice calling out, 'Auntie Carrie...where are you?'

Hurriedly she reached for her bathrobe. Facing Max when Molly was there would be infinitely easier. She could hide behind the child, pretend indifference about last night under the guise of looking after her.

She checked her appearance in the bathroom mirror. Her hair was wet and slicked back from her face and her skin was a little pale. She wished she had some make-up in here, then was cross with herself. It didn't matter what she looked like.

Taking a deep breath, she crossed to the door.

She could hear Molly chatting with Max. 'When are we going to the party?' she was asking him excitedly. 'Will it be soon?'

'You haven't even had breakfast yet,' Carrie said as she stepped into the room.

Molly was standing at the foot of the bed in her pink pyjamas.

'When will we be going, Uncle Max?' Molly looked over at him earnestly.

'We'll be going late this afternoon. After you have had your siesta.' Max didn't prevaricate.

'That's ages away!' Molly wrinkled her nose.

'No, it's not. It will be here before you know it.' Max's eyes connected with Carrie's as she turned.

He looked incredibly handsome in blue jeans and a blue open-necked shirt, and her senses seemed to just dissolve into chaos as she remembered how good his body had felt next to hers. Remembered how easily he had been able to turn her from sane and sensible to wild and wanton.

'Good morning.' He smiled a lazy, attractive smile that made her heartbeats increase even more.

'Morning.' She looked away from him towards her niece. 'Now then, Molly, it's time for your shower. Don't be detaining Uncle Max any longer.' Her voice was brisk and businesslike.

'I'll get off, then,' Max said, and ruffled the child's hair as she started to protest that she didn't want a shower. 'Be good for your auntie Carrie.'

He walked towards the door and then turned back for a moment. 'By the way, I've told my parents that we will arrive a little earlier than everyone else because we have something important to tell them.'

Carrie felt her heart slam fiercely against her chest.

'You'll have to do most of the talking, Max, because I won't know what to say.'

'Yes, you will, you'll be fine.' He smiled at her. 'In fact you'll be more than fine. They will all fall madly in love with you and think you are great.'

Carrie turned away from him. She didn't want everyone—she just wanted him.

CHAPTER TEN

THE sun was climbing higher in the azure-blue sky. And as the temperatures increased the rainwater from the storm last night steamed from the earth in the still morning air.

Carrie was alone with Molly on the terrace. Max had driven Carmel and Bob into the nearby town because they wanted to look around. He was going to drive straight back as Carmel and Bob had said they would get a taxi to Max's parents' house for the party this afternoon. Everything seemed settled. Yet Carrie couldn't relax—all she could think was that the time was ticking nearer and nearer towards meeting Max's family and making their fake engagement public knowledge.

In an effort to take her mind off things she stretched out a hand towards Molly. 'Come on, let's go for a walk in the orchard,' she suggested brightly.

Molly had been playing quietly in the shade, but instantly ran to take hold of her hand, and together they made their way out and down the grassy lane that led towards the grove of citrus trees.

The air was heavy with the scent of lemons and oranges, made fresher by the fact it had rained so heavily in the night, and some of them lay in the long grass.

'Can I have an orange?' Molly asked, stooping to pick one up.

'Yes...but let's get one off the tree.' Carrie reached to pick one. It was harder to take the fruit off the branch than she had thought, and she was struggling to twist it off when a voice said sternly, 'There is a heavy punishment for people caught vandalising fruit trees in this area.'

She turned and saw Max watching them from the shadows of the trees, a glint of humour in his expression that belied the serious tone of his voice.

'Max! You made me jump.' She smiled. 'I didn't expect you back so soon.'

'Well, it's not far into town.' Max strolled across towards them and then smiled at Molly, who looked up at him with a mischievous glint of innocence in her dark eyes.

'Was it you who was vandalising my trees?' he asked.

'No, it was all Auntie Carrie's fault,' Molly told him impishly.

Carrie laughed. 'Thanks a lot, Molly!'

'Fingered by a four-year-old.' Max grinned at her and then reached to take the orange off the tree for them. As he caught hold of the branch he gave it a violent shake, sending a little sprinkling of diamond rainwater washing down from the leaves over them. Molly giggled in delighted surprise.

'I told you there was a penalty for messing with the trees.' Max smiled. He passed the orange over to Molly. 'Shall I take another one off?'

Carrie shook her head. 'No, one is enough. If you give it to me, Molly, I'll peel it for you.'

'I can do it,' Molly said stubbornly, moving ahead of them back out of the shade of the trees.

'Miss Independent,' Carrie observed cheerfully to Max.

'Yes...I wonder where she gets that from.' Max drawled the words with a lazy teasing smile that seemed to set her pulses racing. Then he hurried after Molly. 'Give that orange to me and I'll peel it.'

Carrie smiled as a game ensued, Max chasing Molly around a tree, pretending to catch her and then miss.

The child's laughter filled the air and it made Carrie smile. She walked over to sit down on the low wall that encircled the orchard and watched their antics for a while.

It wasn't long before Max came and sat down beside her. 'I'll catch you later,' he said to Molly as she teasingly came closer, wanting the game to continue.

Carrie turned her face up to the sun and closed her eyes. If this were for real it would be wonderful, she found herself thinking dreamily. Molly was happy around Max…so was she. Swiftly she tried to veer her mind away from that dangerous direction.

'Do you think your parents have any inkling of what we are going to tell them this afternoon?' she asked Max, trying to sound cool and confident.

Max hesitated for a moment. 'I don't think so.'

She glanced over at him. And he grinned at her. 'My father probably won't believe it until he sees it with his own eyes.'

Carrie felt a renewed dart of nervous tension.

'I hope I've brought the right outfit to wear,' she murmured nervously. 'I was just going to put on a summer dress.'

'You could stay the way you are and be perfect,' Max said, his glance flicking down over the white vest top and long floral skirt that she was wearing.

Although the tone of his voice was nonchalant, something about the way his eyes touched her body made her remember the way he had touched her last night, the way her body had responded so vehemently…so passionately. And instantly she felt a scorching stab of pure desire.

'I suppose you are right. It's only a children's party, after all.' Carrie looked away from him hastily and tried to push the memories of last night firmly away. 'It's just that I'm meant to be meeting my future in-laws for the first time. I want to look the part.'

She watched Molly playing happily under the trees, gathering up fallen oranges in the long grass and then piling them up into a pyramid.

'And you will look the part,' Max said confidently. 'Especially if you wear this...'

Carrie looked over at him questioningly and watched as he took a small box out of the pocket of his jeans.

He opened it to reveal a magnificent square-cut diamond engagement ring that sparkled fiercely as the sunlight caught it.

Carrie was so taken aback she didn't know what to say. She glanced from the ring up into Max's eyes.

'Do you like it?' he asked softly.

A warm breeze rustled through the trees, bringing with it the scent of the orchard and the heat of the day.

'It's beautiful,' she said, watching as he took it out of the box.

'Will you do me the honour of wearing it for me?'

Something about the husky way he asked that question made her heart skip violently.

He reached and took hold of her hand, then slowly, yet resolutely, he slipped the ring down onto her finger. The touch of his skin against hers as he gently set it in place on her left hand sent a shiver of poignancy searing straight through her.

'There.' He didn't let go of her hand straight away. 'It's a bit big. You'll have to take it in to the jeweller's to have it made smaller. But it will do for this afternoon.'

'If I have it made smaller it won't be as easy to take it back to the shop,' she murmured, trying desperately to sound composed and cool. But inside she was feeling anything but. Her heart was racing and her emotions were all over the place. Because she wanted this to be for real... she wanted Max so badly that it hurt.

'I don't want to take it back to the shop.' He looked up at her. 'I want you to have the ring.'

'You do?' Her heart seemed to stop beating altogether for a minute.

Max noted how her eyes darkened to a midnight blue...how her skin was pale for a moment.

'Don't worry, it's only make-believe,' he reminded her, a dry edge to his tone. 'I'm not going to hold you to anything.'

'I know that.'

'Good.' He let go of her hand. 'Then we understand each other.'

She nodded. 'Perfectly.'

There was silence between them for a moment. Carrie pretended she was absorbed in watching Molly as she played. But in truth she was acutely conscious of Max's every glance, every move. He seemed to be looking at her very closely and she wondered what he was thinking. She wished he would leave her alone for a while. She needed to gather her senses and throw away the unrealistic wish for this to suddenly turn into a genuine engagement. For Max to look at her with love and desire in his eyes.

Carrie looked down at the engagement ring on her finger. 'So we are going to stick as closely to the truth as possible this afternoon,' she said, trying to turn her mind to the practicalities of the situation. 'We met on a plane coming back from a business trip...'

'Yes...' Max nodded. 'We can even say it was love at first sight.'

'Your mother will like that.' She gave a wry smile. 'It will remind her of her meeting with your dad.'

He smiled back.

'How long do you want to say we've known each other?' she asked, hastily looking away from him again.

'Realistically we could have met about two and a half months ago. I've been flying in and out of Barcelona regularly since then.'

She nodded. 'And what will we say when they ask us about a wedding date?'

'We'll tell them what we told Carmel and Bob. That we're going to sort that out this week.'

He watched as she played with the ring, twisting it around and pulling it up and down on her finger. Then suddenly he reached across and caught hold of her hand, pushing the ring firmly back in place.

'Be careful with that,' he said gently.

'Of course I'll be careful with it.' The touch of his hand instantly threw her senses into chaos.

'You don't want to lose it before the party.'

'I won't lose it.' She glanced down at the diamond. 'I take it it is just a fake?'

He gave a crooked half-smile. 'Of course. It's a fake ring for a fake engagement.'

She nodded. It was only what she had expected. And yet as she looked down at the ring she couldn't help thinking how real it looked. It was exquisitely beautiful. 'It's a very good imitation,' she murmured.

Max stood up from the wall. 'If you don't mind I've got some work to get on with in the vineyard before we leave.'

'No, I don't mind.' She shaded her hand from the sun to look up at him.

'Oh, and I suppose I should tell you that Natasha might be coming to the party this afternoon.' He added the words casually, almost as an afterthought.

'Natasha…as in your former fiancée?' Carrie stared up at him in consternation.

'That's the only Natasha I know,' he said wryly.

'Well…why is she coming to the party?'

'Her mother and father have the neighbouring vineyard, and they are close friends with my parents. As Natasha is back living in Barcelona my mother has extended the invitation to her and her husband, Erick. It's just a courtesy invitation.'

'So they might not come?'

Max paused. 'I think they will. That's why I'm telling you about it up front.'

'I see.' Carrie wished she could see the expression on Max's face, but his back was to the sun and his face was in shadow. 'Will it bother you if she does come?'

Max hesitated for a moment. 'It will be nice to see her again. It must be about two years since we last met up.'

'Is that how long it is since your relationship ended?' Carrie asked curiously.

'No, that happened over four years ago now.' Max raked a hand through his hair in a distracted way, and she sensed suddenly that he didn't want to talk about that.

But Carrie wanted to talk about it; she wanted to know exactly what had happened. She wanted to know every little thing about the relationship, no matter how the facts might disturb her. 'Did you finish with her?' she asked softly.

'Carrie, it's in the past and I'd rather not rake over it,' Max said with finality. 'To be honest with you, I'm trying to forget about it.'

Carrie noted the way he talked about his emotions in the present tense. He was 'trying' to forget about it. If he was truly over Natasha wouldn't he have said he 'had' forgotten about it?

'Anyway, she's very happy now,' Max continued brusquely. 'So you have no need to worry. There will be no bad vibes from Natasha at the party. She's not like that anyway. I can honestly say she is one of the loveliest people I know... You'll like her.'

Carrie doubted that, because it seemed obvious to her that Max wasn't over the other woman; there was still regret in his voice when he spoke of her.

But before she could say anything further Molly interrupted them.

'Look, Uncle Max, look how many oranges I've found.'

Max glanced around at the carefully constructed pyramid. 'Wow, you have been busy,' he said with a smile.

'Will you come and play now?' Molly asked seriously.

Max crouched down so that he was at eye-level with her. 'I can't, Molly, I have some work I must do. But we will have some fun this afternoon at the party, how's that?'

Molly nodded.

'Good girl.' He ruffled her curls affectionately. 'See you later.'

Molly leaned back against the wall and they both watched as Max walked away from them back towards the villa.

'I can't wait for the party,' Molly said happily.

It was only a short car ride from Max's villa to his parents' house.

Molly chattered non-stop in the back of the car, asking Max question after question about the party. Who would be there? What were in the presents that were wrapped so beautifully in gold paper? What would they have to eat? She was so excited that she was hardly able to sit still.

'We're here, Molly.' Max smiled as he turned off the main road and into a driveway that led up towards a large whitewashed farmhouse.

'Is this where you lived when you were little?' Molly asked.

'Yes, that's right.'

'Where did you go to school?'

'I went to the same school that my niece and nephew go to now. It's in a town not far away.'

Carrie liked the way Max answered all of Molly's questions with great patience, never patronising her.

Max had been lucky to grow up somewhere like this, she thought, noting how the red-roofed building nestled snugly in the valley between the wine terraces and the curve of a river that snaked down from the mountains. It was a picturesque scene. The house looked as if it was a part of the rugged landscape, as if it had always been there and quite simply belonged.

Like Max's villa, it was partly covered in bougainvillea, but there the similarity ended. This house had none of Max's villa's sophistication, yet it exuded charm. A black cat slept on a swing chair in the shade of the porch. And at the side of the house a goat was standing in a bed of marigolds, eating his way through the undergrowth.

Max parked his car beside a pick-up truck in the shade of a giant palm tree. 'Looks like we are the first to arrive,' he said to Carrie as they stepped out into the warmth of the afternoon. 'So we will have my parents' undivided attention.'

Carrie suddenly wished that Carmel and Bob would arrive in their taxi, and take some of the emphasis off her. Nervously she brushed an imaginary crease from her blue dress and watched as Molly immediately ran ahead of them to sit on the porch and stroke the cat.

'So we will just stick to the truth as much as possible,' she reiterated quietly to Max as they followed Molly up to the house at a more sedate pace.

'Relax, you'll be fine.' He glanced over at her as if her nervousness amused him.

'What's so funny?' she muttered crossly.

'You are.' He smiled. 'I bet you don't get this edgy when you are dealing with major business contracts.'

Carrie frowned. He was right, she didn't. 'This is different.'

'Is it?' He stopped and reached to catch hold of her hand, pulling her around to face him. 'What's different about it?' he asked softly.

'Well...' Carrie paused. Suddenly she realised what he was getting at. In his eyes this was just a business deal. That was why he was cool and collected. But she had done the unforgivable: she had got carried away with the pretence. She actually cared about what they were doing. No wonder he was looking at her with such questioning eyes. 'Well...I don't have to lie when I'm doing business deals, Max,' she blustered. 'I would have thought that was an obvious difference.'

'You work in advertising, Carrie. You know how to stretch and enhance the truth. You told me that the first time we met...if you remember?'

'I didn't say that.'

'Yes, you did.' He put a hand under her chin, forcing her to keep looking up at him. 'You said that you didn't have to believe in something to sell it.'

'I was talking about products.'

'Well, think of yourself as an assignment, then, and sell yourself.' He gave a crooked grin. 'You won't have to work too hard. You've got the perfect packaging...' he watched the way her skin tinged with a rosy red colour

'...and all the right endorsements...' He reached and caught hold of her hand, turning the diamond so that it caught the light. 'All you will have to do is smile; everyone will love you.'

Everyone except him, she thought, her heart heavy against her chest. He was the only person whose love she sought. Even now, as he talked so coldly of their association like a business deal, she longed for him. Longed to step closer and ask him to just hold her.

She despised herself for the weakness. It had taken her a long time to get over the hurt Martin had caused in her life, and she had been so determined that no one would ever make her feel vulnerable again...and yet here she was years later, her heart on the line again.

The sound of a car pulling up the drive made them both look around. 'It's my sister, Victoria,' Max said, then glanced back at Carrie. 'Just in time to hear our announcement.'

Carrie would have liked to pull away from him. Demand to go home, tell him that she had changed her mind. But she couldn't...

'*Hola*, Max,' Victoria called over to them cheerily. She helped the twins out of the back of the Land Rover before hurrying over towards them, her dark hair swinging in a shiny bob.

She was an attractive woman in her late twenties, slim and petite. She wore a white dress that seemed to float around her as she walked, adding to her air of femininity. 'You're early.' She smiled at Max. 'I hope you've come specially to help Manuel with the cooking.'

She had the same dark eyes as her brother and they shone with warmth and enthusiasm as she reached and kissed Max on both cheeks.

'But of course,' Max said, laughing. 'It wouldn't be a

family party if I didn't cremate a few steaks on the barbecue.' He reached to draw Carrie closer. 'Carrie, I'd like
you to meet my sister, Vickie.'

The girl reached and kissed her on each cheek. 'It's
lovely to meet you,' she said warmly. 'I've already heard
all about you.'

'Have you?' Carrie glanced in surprise up at Max.

'Not from him. From the font of all knowledge,
Estelle.' Victoria laughed. Then looked past her as Molly
came down the steps and stood close behind Carrie.

'This is Molly,' Carrie said, trying to bring the child
forward. But Molly was stubbornly hiding behind her.
'Aren't you going to say hello to Max's sister?' Carrie
asked gently. 'And look, this is Belle and Emilio—you
must wish them a happy birthday.'

Molly peeped around at the children, but seemed suddenly struck dumb with shyness.

'Happy birthday.' Carrie smiled at the twins. They
looked adorable. Belle had a pale yellow dress on and
Emilio was wearing denim jeans and a smart white shirt.

'We have a birthday present for you in the back of the
car,' Max said. And suddenly their angelic silence was
broken with boisterous chatter as they launched themselves at their uncle to ask him excitedly what he had got
for them. Molly stepped forward, her shyness suddenly
forgotten as she watched the way the other children were
leaping around in anticipation.

'Go and show Belle and Emilio where their birthday
present is in the car, Molly.' Max smiled over at her. 'On
the back seat.'

Immediately the three children were running down towards Max's vehicle as if they had known each other for
years, Molly full of self-importance because she knew

where the presents where and what was inside the gold paper.

'The peace and quiet didn't last for long.' Victoria smiled. 'I just hope they can keep their clothes clean until at least a few other people have arrived...' She trailed off as she suddenly noticed the engagement ring on Carrie's finger. 'Is that...?' She looked questioningly up at Carrie and then over towards Max. 'You're not...?'

'Yes.' Max smiled. 'We were just on our way in to give the good news.'

Victoria squealed with excitement. 'I can't believe you have stood there and rattled on about children's presents—we should be inside... Oh, congratulations...' She kissed Carrie, then flung her arms around her brother, her pleasure almost outweighing the children's a few moments ago. 'This is wonderful, Max...everyone is going to be thrilled.'

Carrie found herself being half pulled by the girl, up and through the front door.

It was dark inside, and she had only a vague impression of a beautiful hallway with rush mats on a stone floor, pine country antiques and squashy butter-gold furniture in a wide, spacious lounge. Victoria led her through the rooms at a pace, not stopping for a moment until they were outside onto a balcony that overlooked the river and the valley beyond.

Victoria's husband Manuel was out there, lighting the barbecue, and a woman of about sixty was chopping vegetables on a counter beside him.

'*Mamá*, wonderful news,' Victoria said as she presented Carrie with a flourish. 'You'll never guess...'

The woman turned and Carrie saw that she was very attractive and petite, with dark hair silvering around the temples. She took off the apron she had over her floral dress and came towards them immediately.

'Max has got engaged! This is Carrie, *Mamá*—your future daughter-in-law.'

Carrie needn't have worried about what she was going to say; everyone suddenly seemed to be talking all at once. Max's mother was ecstatic; she hugged Carrie and then flung her arms around Max.

'I knew there was something different with you just recently...knew there was something afoot—you've looked so happy! I'm so pleased for you both. Where is your father, Max? He should be here!'

A bottle of champagne was produced. Then Max's father appeared in the doorway and was told the news.

Carrie noted that Max was very like his dad; he was tall and well built, with hair that was still thick and dark. He looked over at his son sceptically as he heard the news. 'You're settling down here...or are you heading back to Seville?'

'I'm giving up my job in Seville, Father, and making my home here,' Max told him steadily. 'I told you that last week.'

'Yes, you did. But last week I couldn't see what had changed to make you want to stay here.' Max's dad looked over at Carrie and then he smiled. 'But I understand now.'

As he came across and gave Carrie a hug she felt overwhelmed with the warmth and affection that seemed to surround her.

The door opened and more of Max's relatives arrived. She was introduced to aunts and uncles, to cousins and second cousins, and after a while she was lost with the amount of names she was trying to remember.

Molly ran in with Emilio and Belle, and Max swept her

up into his arms as she passed and brought her over to introduce her to his mum and dad.

Carrie watched across the crowded room as Max's mother sat the child on her knee and started to talk to her. Molly seemed to have got over her earlier bout of shyness because she appeared to be chatting back quite happily.

Carmel and Bob arrived, and Carrie excused herself from the crowd around her to go and speak to them. But by the time she had got across the patio Max had already introduced them to his parents and they were deep in conversation.

'I believe you've got your ring,' Carmel said, and took hold of Carrie's hand to look. 'It's beautiful, my dear,' she said softly. 'I'm so happy for you.'

'We are going to have to get these two up the aisle quickly then, Carmel,' Max's mother said with a smile. 'Before you and Bob have to go back home.'

'We'd really like that,' Carmel said, and sat down on the seat next to her. 'They make a lovely couple, don't they?'

Everywhere Carrie moved in the room she could hear people complimenting them and wishing them well. If only they knew, she thought as she glanced over to where Max was deep in conversation with his father. That this was all a charade...

Across the patio she saw Estelle and her husband Ambrosio had arrived. Estelle's eyes connected with hers across the room and then she raised her glass of wine in a salute that seemed vaguely mocking somehow.

Carrie had the distinct impression that the woman was saying to her, You may be fooling everyone else in this room, but not me. I know the truth. Hurriedly Carrie looked away from her. Victoria might have referred to

Estelle as the 'font of all knowledge', but even Estelle couldn't possibly know the truth.

Or could she?

Because as Carrie's gaze moved back towards Max she noticed that he was barely listening to his father now; his attention had been distracted by a woman who was standing just beside the patio doors.

Carrie didn't need anyone to tell her that the woman was Natasha. The look on Max's face told her that quite clearly.

CHAPTER ELEVEN

NATASHA was even more beautiful than Carrie had imagined. She was in her mid-thirties and had short dark hair that was expertly cut, flattering the classical shape of her face, emphasising her high cheekbones and huge blue eyes. The closely fitted halter-neck top and white trousers that she wore did nothing to disguise the fact that she was heavily pregnant; in fact they deliberately seemed to draw attention to the large bump, making it clear at the same time that once the baby was born she would be reed-slim.

She seemed to radiate a healthy vitality that shone from her blue eyes, and every now and then as people spoke to her she placed a hand on her stomach.

Carrie was surprised the woman was pregnant. Maybe she had the wrong person. Maybe this wasn't Natasha. Max hadn't mentioned she was expecting—unless, of course, Max hadn't known.

She glanced back at him. He was still watching her and Carrie thought she saw a flicker of regret in his eyes as he watched her happily showing off her pregnancy. She took a sip of her champagne and told herself that she was imagining things…and anyway she didn't care.

But as Max excused himself from his parents to walk purposefully in the other woman's direction the sick feeling of jealousy caught her off guard.

Natasha looked pleased to see him; she kissed him on each cheek and then looked up at him with a shy expression in her eyes. Obviously Max was talking to her about her pregnancy, because she put her hand on her stomach and smiled. Then she caught hold of Max's hand and placed it on her stomach as well.

The sick feeling inside Carrie suddenly turned to a red-hot wave of anger. She wanted to go across and physically drag Max away from her...how dared he touch her like that?

'Everything all right, Carrie?'

Carrie looked around and to her dismay saw Estelle standing beside her. 'Yes, fine, thanks.' She gritted her teeth and smiled. Estelle was the last person she wanted to have to deal with right now.

'Congratulations, by the way. And it's a lovely ring.'

'Thanks.' Carrie looked down at the sparkle of her engagement ring. She had no right to be angry with Max, she told herself fiercely. The ring wasn't real...the engagement wasn't real. If he was still holding a torch for Natasha, then that was his problem, and it was nothing to do with her. Max was free to flirt and laugh with whatever woman he liked.

Yet the sensible words didn't make her feel any better.

'Have you set a date for the wedding yet?' Estelle asked.

'No, not yet.' Carrie couldn't stop herself looking across at Max again. He was still talking to Natasha. They seemed perfectly at ease together, laughing as if at some private joke.

'Natasha's husband is conspicuous by his absence,' Estelle said, following her gaze. 'I'm sure Natasha wouldn't be able to flirt quite so openly with Max if Erick was here.'

Carrie looked away from the couple hurriedly. 'They are just old friends, Estelle,' she said firmly.

'If you say so.' Estelle gave her a somewhat brittle smile. 'Anyway, good luck with your forthcoming marriage,' she murmured, her tone clearly indicating that she would definitely be in need of luck to make things work.

Before Carrie could say anything else to her the woman turned away to resume a conversation with someone else.

Carrie walked in the opposite direction, trying to keep her back firmly towards Max. She didn't want anyone else to notice how much it bothered her to see him and his ex-lover in such cosy harmony.

Manuel was throwing chicken on the barbecue, and next to him Ambrosio was setting up a trestle-table full of food. 'Can I be of any help?' Carrie asked, hoping the answer would be yes; she felt as if she needed to do something to take her mind away from Natasha.

'No, everything is under control. I've got the expert here to help.' Manuel grinned over at Ambrosio.

'This is supposed to be my time off,' Ambrosio complained, and then laughed when Carrie told him she wouldn't mind taking over.

'No, I don't mind doing this…I enjoy it, really. Where has that fiancé of yours got to?'

'I don't know. He's…over talking to Natasha, I think.' Carrie very carefully tried to sound as if she didn't care.

'Is he?' Ambrosio shook his head.

Did he think Max was still in love with Natasha as well? Carrie wondered suddenly. Somehow Estelle's barbed remarks were easier to bear. Carrie could shrug her off as just being a bitch…but Ambrosio—that was different.

'Are you sure I can't help?' Carrie asked again, determined to squash the feelings of jealousy inside her.

'No, go and enjoy yourself.' Manuel reached for a bottle of champagne and before she could stop him he topped up her glass.

The light of the day was starting to fade, the sun sinking

quickly below the mountains. Down in the garden Carrie could see Molly, running around amongst a crowd of children; their laughter drifted upwards in the stillness of the air. Victoria was with them and it looked as if she was trying to organise them into teams...

Molly looked around, as if she sensed Carrie watching her, and waved happily.

Carrie waved back.

Somebody had put some music on and a few people were dancing on the smaller patio. Low-level lighting flickered on around the garden.

'Here you are.' Max's voice coming from behind her took her by surprise. 'I wondered where you were hiding.'

Carrie wanted to say, Weren't you the one who was hiding from me? Laughing and flirting with your ex-lover. The words burnt inside her, but she knew she had no right to say them so she bit her tongue.

'Shall we have a dance?' He put his arm around her waist. The touch of his hand seemed to sear through her. It filled her with a weakness that she despised herself for.

'I'd rather not, Max,' she said quickly, trying to pull herself away from him.

But he didn't let go of her; instead he pulled her even closer. 'Hey, we have got to keep up appearances here.' He murmured the words huskily against her ear. 'I must have at least one dance with my fiancée.'

'Max, I...' But before she could say anything else he took the glass of champagne from her hand and put it down on a side table before leading her firmly towards the other patio.

The music was slow and romantic and Carrie was forced to move closer into his arms; it was either that or create a scene.

'It's all going very well so far, don't you think?' Max's

voice was close to her ear and it sent shivers of desire racing through her.

'Do you think so?' Her voice was cool and she tried desperately not to allow her body to relax against his.

'Yes. I told you, you had nothing to worry about; my parents think you are wonderful. In fact you have wowed everyone.'

At his words a feeling of guilt stole through her. Carrie didn't want to deceive these people. She liked Max's parents, and she didn't want to lie to them—she didn't want to lie to anyone. She wished she had never agreed to this charade and it was all her fault. She had started all this when she had asked Max to pose as her fiancé.

Carrie tried to move away from him, but he held her close. She wished that she could rid herself of the treacherous feelings of desire that flooded through her at his nearness. Her body seemed to respond to him of its own volition; even the scent of his cologne disturbed her senses, bringing back vivid memories of their lovemaking last night. She felt her stomach contract with longing, felt butterflies surging through her system; fiercely she tried to push those feelings away.

'Max...' she looked up at him, her eyes wide and pleading '...this is all wrong...'

'This is very right,' he said, a small smile curving his lips. 'In fact nothing has ever felt so right.'

She frowned, her heart skipping several beats, wondering what he meant. Then he leaned down and suddenly his lips were covering hers in a kiss that sent her dizzying emotions into even further chaos. She wound her arms up and around his shoulders, loving the feel of him so close, wanting the kiss to go on and on for ever.

He pulled away and smiled at her. It was a few moments before she realised that they were suddenly the centre of attention and that people had gathered around the dance floor to applaud them.

Looking around at the mass of faces, all smiling, all wishing them well for the future, Carrie realised why Max had kissed her...why he had said this was right. He was playing to the audience, it was just another strand in the web of deceit.

Suddenly she knew that she couldn't take this any longer. Couldn't stand here and lie for one minute more.

'Max, I need to get out of here.' She pulled away from him, her voice barely audible. Her breathing came in short, sharp stabs as she fought to get herself under control.

She saw the way his eyes darkened, the way he frowned.

'I'm sorry...' She pulled away from him before she lost the strength to do so.

No one seemed to notice her distress. People smiled at her and patted her on the back as she hurried past them.

It was a relief to get out into the shadows of the garden, away from prying eyes. She could feel the hot prickle of tears building up inside her.

'Carrie, what's wrong?' Max caught up with her almost immediately. He put a hand on her shoulder and tried to turn her to face him.

'Don't, Max.' Stubbornly she refused to turn. She didn't want him to see her crying.

'What is it, *querida*...? You're doing wonderfully well, and there's nothing to worry about.'

The gentleness of his tone made anger rise to her defence. 'Nothing to worry about?' she repeated his words fiercely and then spun around to look up at him. 'Well, I suppose you would think that, wouldn't you? Because, let's face it, all this deceit comes easily to you. I just wish it came as easily to me. I feel like a monster, lying to your family like this…'

'Carrie, you are being silly, calm down—'

'No, I won't calm down, Max.' She cut across his soothing words and moved back a step as he reached to touch her. 'Not only are you lying glibly to people who care about you, but you are using me and I don't like it.'

'I'm not using you, Carrie,' he said softly, his gaze raking over the pallor of her skin in the moonlight, the fierce glitter of tears in her eyes.

'Of course you are using me! You couldn't care less about my feelings. All you care about is the end result.'

'I thought that was what you cared about…what you wanted.' He said the words quietly. 'No emotional strings…just a straightforward business deal. You get Molly; I smooth things over with my father.'

He seemed to be looking at her with such intensity that she felt he could see straight through to the truth. That he could guess the strength of her feelings for him. The idea was horrifying… She had her pride, after all, and he would probably find it extremely amusing to know that she was in love with him. 'It was what I wanted,' she said firmly.

'*Was?*'

'I mean…it *is* what I want.' Mortified, Carrie raked a hand through her hair. 'You're confusing me, Max.'

'Am I?' He took a step forward, a smile curving the sensual lips.

'I know we had an agreement. I know I said I'd go along with the charade. But I didn't realise then just how it would feel…' She trailed off helplessly.

'And how does it feel?' he prompted softly.

'It feels terrible.' She glared up at him. 'I hate it. I hate the pretence. I hate the way you can turn on that charm and lie through your teeth, the way you can dance with me as if you have feelings for me. Kiss me as if it means something…' Her voice caught slightly, before she pulled herself together to continue angrily. 'And all the time you are lying to your parents…and everyone back in there—' she waved helplessly in the direction of the house '—when everyone has been so wonderfully kind and so happy for us. We are such frauds…how can we do this to them?'

'It's a means to an end—'

'Well, I'm sorry, I can't go through with this any more…' She cut across his calm reasoning heatedly. 'I can't be as emotionally detached as you seem to be.' Her voice broke slightly.

'Can't you?'

It was strange—she had thought Max would be angry when she said that, but he didn't sound even slightly annoyed; in fact there was a stillness about him, a watchfulness that was hard to gauge.

'I know you are worried about your father's health,' she continued hurriedly. 'But the end does not justify the means. You are lying to the people closest to you…people who care about your future—and the awful thing is, it is probably all my fault. I started all this but I can't be an accomplice to it any more, Max.' Her eyes darkened suddenly with pain. 'You don't love me—'

'Ah, but I do,' he cut across her quietly.

The words stunned her into silence and she looked up at him, wondering if she had imagined them. Maybe she wanted to hear him say he loved her so desperately that she was hallucinating.

'I think I've loved you from the first moment I sat next to you on that plane and looked across into your eyes,' he continued.

'You don't really mean that?' Her voice was huskily unsure.

'I mean it with all of my heart...' he answered softly. 'From the first moment we met I was captivated by you, and I couldn't believe my luck when I saw those business papers in front of you with Santos Wines on them. It was as if destiny had brought us together.' He reached out and stroked a strand of her hair back from her face with a tender hand. 'I knew that you didn't feel the same about me, so the opportunity to step in as your fake fiancé was heaven-sent. And I was hoping that if we let this engagement continue that, given time, you'd come to love me.'

Tears spilled down her cheeks. She could hardly believe what he was saying to her.

'Don't cry, *querida*,' he said gently. 'I wouldn't be saying all this to you except for the fact that your anger and your words just now have offered me a shred of hope that maybe you do have feelings for me.'

'I'm crying because I'm so happy, Max.' Her voice was a mere whisper in the stillness of the air. 'I do have feelings for you. That's the main reason I felt I couldn't continue with this phoney engagement. Max, I love you so much that it hurts.'

Max reached out a tender hand and brushed her tears away, a look of rapture on his face. 'Up until a few moments ago I hardly dared hope that you would ever say that to me...' Then he bent his head and his lips found hers in a possessive kiss that made all rational thought disappear. The sensation of pure need that instantly sprang to life inside her was shockingly intense.

She kissed him back with long, lingering, intense pleasure.

'This feels like a dream,' Carrie murmured unsteadily as he pulled back.

'For me too,' Max murmured. 'Last night when I held you in my arms it was the most wonderful night of my life, and I longed to tell you exactly how I felt, but I didn't dare in case I scared you away.'

'And I thought that last night meant nothing to you...' Her voice lowered as she remembered the pain of those feelings. 'I thought it was just a casual fling as far as you were concerned.'

Max shook his head. 'I've never felt this deeply, this passionately about anyone in all my life. When I hold you in my arms, when we kiss it's the most wonderful feeling. I had to force myself to leave you this morning because I knew if I stayed in your bed I'd end up pouring my heart out and I didn't think it was what you wanted to hear. I've kept telling myself that I have to be patient. That you have been hurt in the past and I need to take things slowly.'

'Oh, Max, you are not just saying all this, are you?' she asked him tentatively, scared because these were all the things she had wanted to hear.

He looked down into her eyes, so wide and filled with hope. 'I know you think I can tell lies with glib ease, but I assure you, Carrie, my feelings for you are genuine. Yes, I have been worried about my father's health and I've wanted to reassure him of my intentions, but I have never said anything to my parents—or to Carmel and Bob, for that matter—that I haven't felt deeply...' he caught hold of her hand and placed it over his heart '...right about here.'

'You really love me?' She looked up at him wonderingly. There was no doubting the depth of sincerity in his voice, in his eyes.

'Deeply and madly.' He smiled at her, a crooked half-smile that sent her senses spinning wildly with happiness.

He pulled her close, holding her in a bear-like hug. 'You mean everything to me, *querida*. And if you will just give me a chance I want to spend the rest of my life proving that to you...'

She cuddled closer to him, breathing in the scent of his cologne; the pleasure of being held, of hearing him saying such wonderful things, was incredibly intense.

'Just a few moments ago I truly believed that you were still holding a torch for Natasha.'

Max pulled back from her slightly and looked genuinely startled at that. 'Natasha is a dear friend, Carrie, but I have never felt about her—or anyone else—the way I do about you. Natasha and I didn't love each other enough—there was no real spark. We kind of just drifted together because it was expected of us. That's why our engagement didn't work.'

'But I was watching you as you talked to her about her pregnancy and you seemed almost wistful...'

'If I was wistful it was because I was thinking how much I'd like to have a baby with you. For you, me and Molly to be a real family.'

'Oh, Max...' She wound her arms up around his neck, pressing her body close against his...so close that she wanted to melt into him. 'That's what I want too.' Her voice broke huskily, and then suddenly they were kissing again, fierce, urgent kisses as if they couldn't get enough of each other. Couldn't get close enough.

'You don't know how often I've dreamt of you saying that to me.' His voice tickled against her ear as he kissed the side of her neck and then her cheek before capturing her lips again. 'My beautiful, darling Carrie...'

He lifted her off her feet and spun her around. 'Tell me again that you love me,' he demanded in a laughing yet **fiercely possessive tone.**

She buried her head against his chest, feeling dizzy and light-headed, but it wasn't from the way he was spinning her around, it was with sheer happiness. 'I love you with all my heart, Max. In fact I think if I loved you any more my heart would burst with pure overloaded joy,' she said breathlessly.

He stopped spinning her around and tipped her chin up to look gently into her eyes. 'And I adore you, and that is the way it will stay, *querida*.'

'Auntie Carrie, Uncle Max!' Molly interrupted them, her little voice filled with excitement. 'Look what I've won in the games.'

It took a moment for them to pull apart and look down at the little girl. She held up a doll to show them, her eyes bright with happiness.

Max turned and with one swoop lifted her up into his arms. 'That's wonderful, sweetheart. And I'm glad you are here because Auntie Carrie and I have something to ask you.' He reached out and pulled Carrie closer, so that the three of them were enclosed tightly in their own little circle.

'How would you like to be a flower girl at our wedding?'

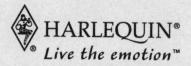

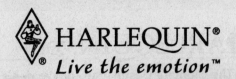

HARLEQUIN®
Live the emotion™

Upbeat,
All-American Romances

flipside

Romantic Comedy

Harlequin Historicals®

Historical,
Romantic Adventure

INTRIGUE

Romantic Suspense

HARLEQUIN ROMANCE®

The essence of
modern romance

Seduction and passion
guaranteed

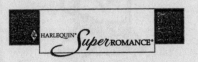

Emotional,
Exciting, Unexpected

Sassy, Sexy, Seductive!

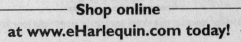

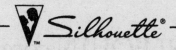